Published by *featherproof* Books and Moniker Records

First edition
10 9 8 7 6 5 4 3 2 1

Library of Congress Control Number: 2016959330
ISBN 13: 9781943888092

Edited by Tim Kinsella
Cover Illustration by Aleksandra Furman
Design by Zach Dodson
Set in Garamond Condensed

Printed in the United States of America

From the Inside

By John Henry Timmis IV
1989

From the inside

By John Henry Timmis IV

1989

"Beyond the fiction of reality, there is the reality of the fiction."

—Slavoj Žižek, *Less Than Nothing: Hegel and the Shadow of Dialectical Materialism*

Introduction

By Plastic Crimewave

There's a completely ridiculous moment in the memoir of glam-punk rocker John Henry Timmis IV—aka JT IV—in which he's undergoing a "brainwave test," and in order to throw off the results, he imagines Jimmy Page guitar solos in his head. John saw that the "patterns went crazy" on the charts as he imagined them, and somehow I imagined John laughing down at me from his dirty DIY cloud in the sky—happy that he was, in fact, making my own head go a bit round the bend trying to read between the lines of his tell-all biography.

John idolized Lou Reed, and once I saw a Reed interview where the interviewer was like, "well, this such-and-such a thing happened to you." And Reed answered, "No, that happened to Lou Reed. You're talking to Louis Reed"—ie, Reed could distinguish between his personas. Similarly, John Henry Timmis IV is clearly trying to build his own legend, self-aware of cultivating his outsider persona.

Or was he??? Obviously there's possibly a chance that maybe some of this is embellished; the grandstanding opinions, and some of the sexy passages seem to slide back and forth between intense confessional and fantasy. Did a guy really jizz on his face? Was he really locked in this institution that two members of Kansas had been to? Was he really held in the exact same cell in which James Taylor wrote "Fire and Rain?" What mythos does that create? Why make that up? Also, if he really was abused and all of this other terrible stuff, then he is revealing everything, but he could also be making that stuff up to build up this persona. Even if he just thought it was cool to be in gay orgies for money, there's still something that John reveals by choosing that image. His surviving family members never responded to attempts to confirm or deny any facts of the story. There are no close friends left to track down to get the real story. There's really only this document of his mythos.

My all-time favorite movie is the absolutely demolishing fucked-up-kids tour-de-force *Over the Edge* (notable to some for being Matt Dillon's 1st movie, where he wears a crop-top T.) JT IV was the REAL *Over The Edge* kid. Sure, the Over the Edge soundtrack has Cheap Trick and Van Halen, and John was more into Alice Cooper. But basically, there's an audience—fans of classic juvenile delinquency tales—waiting for this book that doesn't even know it.

I was transported back to when I first fell in love with JT IV via THE MUSIC. I guess I first heard the "Destructo Rock" single on a compilation,"Staring Down The Barrel," a kind of a "Killed by Death" punk-style compilation. I thought it was pretty savage, sludgy and cool, but I didn't make the connection that he was from the Chicago area and I'd never heard his full LP (which I later found out had originally been mastered at the wrong speed). Robert Manis, who had "discovered" the band Death, approached me about reissuing JT IV's album on my new Galactic Zoo Disk imprint on Drag City Records in 2008. Robert put it all together and it friggin blew me away.

The punkier, proto-grunge stuff was about 10 years ahead of its time, before Mudhoney, Tad, and Nirvana's Bleach. But there was also this raw glam-punk, and mournful folkier songs like "In The Can" and "Out Of The Can" that I would almost put in the "acid-folk" genre—but JT's singing about stuff like prison and turning tricks, making it sort of downer junky-folk? Like the recently-celebrated Rodriguez, the music is pretty and even gentle, but the lyrics have a bleak urban blight vibe to them. Shit, there was even a novelty song about the CTA? Each song gave you a different aspect of John's personality.

And the DVD that came with the record included these homemade videos, like John in a Frankenstein mask singing "In Every Dream Home a Heartache" by Roxy Music; with a bad 80's video font exclaiming—*This is John Henry Timmis after being up for Eight days*. He was clearly living the life he sang about, or at least he wanted you to think that he was. The Timmis mind-fuck continues. The videos revealed that JT IV could actually shred! He was a much better guitar player than you'd know from his punkish songs. And he liked to cover the Beatles and Simon and Garfunkel? (Or am I just spreading a myth, hmm.) In later videos he's a little heavier, and a little burned out, with a dangly earring, and you can see that maybe he kind of bottomed out. This book is written 13 years before his death, reflecting back on his life 13 before that. Or was it?

Like myself, John was a good old working class Midwestern boy, just at times forced into froofy places, the world of The Monkees' "Pleasant Valley Sunday," and he was troubled by self-loathing over this. He needed to escape New Grenada (the planned community in Over The Edge that needed to be blown to bits.) But where to? Oddly, where my fam often 'escaped' to, Lake Geneva,

Wisconsin, which came to represent a utopia to John, the tourist town where anything goes, and he could possibly gay-hustle and score drugs.

Like Mick Jones from the Clash worshipped Mott the Hoople and Steve Jones from the Sex Pistols worshipped T-Rex, John idolized Bowie and the glam one-man-against-the-world kind of thing. But also like myself, he was also a total classic rock nerd, which did not fly with most of the punks, who saw say, Led Zeppelin, as a bloated dinosaur. Maybe John took glam androgyny to full blown bisexuality, but even if he didn't really do that stuff, he was truly responding to Bowie's bigger mission, which was all about breaking out of this straight-world thing. He made it cool to be bisexual. Most Bowie fans were just putting a lightning bolt on their face at best.

It's odd that the book doesn't go into how John recorded the music. It's more about him as a person than him as a musician. He talks way more about shopping his records around than he does about actually recording them, yet he supposedly spent $11,000 to make his "concert movie," which looks to have used one camcorder in a big empty hall. MYSTERIOUS. And he brags that his drummer is the fastest conga player in the world...how the hell would you gauge that?

We all love reading about punks who wanna stick it to everyone. It's pure id and it's important to go through that at some point in life. Still, John ended up working for the police, raising money for the fraternal order. Sure, maybe he got tired of being arrested constantly, and he's taking care of his girlfriend's child. But for all his stick-to-the-man ethics there's a certain level where John is malleable, and that disillusionment is part of "growing up" for everyone I guess.

John name drops *One Flew Over The Cuckoo's Nest*, so maybe he is just writing a novel here, and a few clunky things do seem to give him away. Like the nurse—*and then she gave me a massage. It was the best massage*—that's like a weird unrealized fantasy of a kid: "what do adults do to each other?" "Well, they massage each other, and it feels good." The stilted speeches that people give him, like the doctor—*and he said listen, son*—it's not the way people talk at all. The structure, the framing that he overshoots, is clumsy. And John sums it all up a little too pat at the end with his personal philosophy manifesto on life. These naive and amateur moves make the book both earnest and comfortably fitting within the expectations of the genre. Even the way he describes the rich kids that don't seem crazy, but their parents send them to The Menninger Foundation to get rid of them, that's part of the mythology with those sorts of places, an offshoot of the teen rebellion genre. Like Bad Boys with Sean Penn, the harsh ones are cathartic for people because at the end you turn it off and *thank god I don't have to be in there*.

JT is almost like a Manson figure: *I'm your garbage, a mirror of society, the effect of societal problems, I'm the dark part of society you don't want to acknowledge. The forgotten son of your modern paradigm.*

He doesn't actually ever talk about punk, the genre he's most closely associated with. Either he never encountered it, or it wasn't important to him. Like most punks, he took classic rock and honed in on the elements that spoke to him. Like an alternate dimension, parallel to known rock history, he was in line with what was going on in Cleveland in the mid-to-late 70s, like Rocket from the Tombs and The Mirrors, who weren't necessarily influenced by punk rock, but by the Velvet Underground, weird glam, and hard rock and mutated into what basically came out sounding like punk rock, because those were the same key components.

Each chapter centers around a different lady, and maybe a bit one-dimensionally, one is synonymous with sex, one with nurturing, one is as damaged as him, and there's even the poor little rich girl. Yet, he respects women—maybe uncommonly so for the time. He is very loving and respectful toward most of them. There are no mere "muses" for his music or tale. Ok, of course they're all beautiful and tragic, and they all love him and his piercing eyes. Yet while John mainly identifies as being straight, he clearly acknowledges his other tendencies in a way that was pretty no-BS and progressive for the time.

All these thoughts hit me as I read John's real or exaggerated adventures. I thought of the many friends I've had over the years who've been obsessed with the history and representation of juvenile delinquency (some also no longer with us, sadly). And I thought also of my pals that were weird-punk obsessives aka the "Killed by Death crowd" or even the "Ugly Things music historian crowd"—a few of which who are also no longer with us. These obsessions often blur to become their own reality or perceived reality. This book is for them, but maybe really for any teenager, so they can vicariously live out a rebellious existence through these danger-ridden fantasies, or perhaps to inspire them to live recklessly and free and to give us more pure, yet tragic, artistes like John Henry Timmis IV.

To my good friend Lee Groban

Foreward

Throughout the years since the Menninger Foundation opened its doors, there have been countless books written by the so-called "professionals" who work there. More books came from psychologists around the world who looked to Menninger's for advice. Even Truman Capote credited the foundation with helping him build a profile of the killers for his bestseller titled *In Cold Blood*. These accounts all convey the positive aspects of the mental health care system, and Menninger's has grown to become the most respected institution in the world.

Until now, no insider or "patient" has ever told the truth about what goes on behind those locked doors. I was held there against my will for two and a half years after being diagnosed as a "psychopath." The stories I have to tell about that experience will probably amaze you. This book could turn out to be quite controversial when it is published because a lot of people in high places will not like what I have to say. But to them I say what they always used to tell me: "The truth is sometimes painful." I feel it is important that this story finally be told, not only for my personal peace of mind, but so that the public will comprehend the problems facing everyone involved with the subject of clinical psychology and psychiatry.

I would also like to dedicate this work to Rachel Couenneoeur, a former social worker at Menninger's, and the only person who was able to help me even though the odds were against us from the start. I hope someday she will read this and feel good about her contribution to my life. Rachel, I still love you.

Chapter one

The Menninger Foundation is a psychiatric care facility located in the heart of America: Topeka, Kansas. It sits on about thirty acres of land surrounded by a cemetery, a highway, and a zoo. Driving into the place, it has a strangely pleasant atmosphere which hides the pain and mental torture that goes on there year after year. The grounds have large trees and a nice landscape job. I was brought there as a juvenile in 1976 after running away from home and being arrested numerous times for various crimes like possession of marijuana, disorderly conduct, prostitution, and robbery. I was admitted to the institution on the same day as another angry young man who had just murdered his mother, father, and sister by shooting them all at point blank range with a shotgun. He was released a year and a half before me.

I had been diagnosed as a psychopath at Evanston Hospital in Illinois. Now, I was being transferred to Menninger's for a more in-depth examination to figure out what treatment would be "best" for me. I was a troubled youth who longed to grow up and be out from under the thumbs of all the authority figures around me. If you do not conform to the norms of society, they will put you away and treat you like a common criminal. And from these criminals, you will learn how to be a criminal. It's a great education, all right.

But through a bizarre set of circumstances, I ended up in the psychiatric care system instead of the criminal system because my parents were rich and supposedly wanted the best for me.

Menninger's was the most high-class institution of its type, or so I was told. Johnny Carson went there to straighten out his head during troubled times. The Shah of Iran left his son there for safekeeping. James Taylor wrote "Fire and Rain" in the same cell as I was in, but we were there at different times. Two members of the million-selling rock group Kansas were there under the care of my psychiatrist, Dr. Petersen. Such was the true folklore of the place. I was unimpressed. I wanted to be free.

They searched through all my personal belongings when I got there, but I still managed to smuggle in six grams of Lebanese hash, and that kept my spirits up for the first couple of weeks until it was gone. I did not know how long I would be there. You see, under this system there is no set time limit on punishment for a specific crime. They can keep you until they declare that you are cured, which they hardly ever do for fear of legal retribution if someone they've released flips out and goes on a rampage. The entire time I was there, only five people were released as "cured." Strangely enough, the guy who murdered his whole family in cold blood was one of them.

The general plan of action was that I would undergo a six week examination. After that I could be subject to as much as three years' treatment. It felt to me almost like I was getting the death sentence. That is a long time to take out of a young person's life. But my parents could foot the bills.

The first night I was on the ward there, a sixteen-year-old girl who was very attractive tried to commit suicide by slashing her wrists with some broken glass from a Coke bottle. The goons in white coats saved her life, then strapped her down to her bed and injected her with drugs. I bet that made her very happy to be alive. As you can see, it was insanity from the beginning.

The first day I was there, I was shown my lovely room, which was actually a cell with bulletproof glass. My parents bid me farewell, telling me they'd be back in six weeks for the results of the tests and for some scheduled group meetings between me, them, and the doctors. My parents showed little emotion as they left me there. It was like they were glad to get rid of me. Now they could go make love on the beach in the Cayman Islands and forget all about me. I was well taken care of.

On the second day I was there, they subjected me to a brainwave test in which electrodes were fastened to my head. Impulses in my head were recorded on paper by a machine that converted brainwaves into patterns. It is then easy for the doctors to spot a psychological disorder if there are abnormalities in the patterns. But some people, like me, can throw the machine off by thinking about music. I was thinking about the soundtrack to Led Zeppelin's *The Song Remains the Same* while taking the test. Jimmy Page's wild guitar solos turned up on paper as static indicating some sort of disorder. I looked over the printed readout and saw that the patterns went crazy at the times when I was playing the intense parts of songs through my head.

On the third day, they gave me the standard inkblot test in which I was to tell them what shapeless images reminded me of. I said, for example, "That looks to me like three elephants making love to a men's glee club." I was being rebellious, giving ridiculous answers that they appeared to be taking seriously. They wrote down everything I said in their log books, and I felt like an insect being probed under a microscope. I was just as rebellious during the word association test, when the doctor would say one word and I had to reply with the first other word that popped into my brain. The female psychologist whose name I can't remember, she got a kick out of saying words like 'vagina' or 'breast,' to which I would jokingly answer 'rape' or 'murder.' I figured I had nothing left to lose. I was already locked up. The worst was over. Why not toy with these fools and play games with them? There was no sincerity whatsoever in my answers to the word association test. Still, again they seemed to take me very seriously. I did myself great harm by acting out in this fashion. Menninger's was basing their evaluation and recommendation on the results of these tests. Consequently, they declared that I was a "psychopath with schizophrenic overtones, in need of two to three years treatment," otherwise I was "on the path to self destruction, perhaps suicide."

Suicide was the farthest thing from my mind. I wanted to get out and live, live, LIVE!!! It felt so bad to have my freedom taken away. I found myself filled with hate, and the need to get revenge on those who had put me there. I still believe to this day that there was really nothing wrong with me. I did not belong there. But read on and judge for yourselves as the plot thickens.

On the fourth day I went to my first group meeting. It included all of the doctors and social workers on the ward, plus all of the patients. One was retarded, another had cerebral palsy, both of them boys. The other ten patients were young people like myself, juvenile delinquents at the end of the road. The vibe of depression in the air was almost overwhelming. The girls cried and the boys begged for mercy, but I sat there stone-faced without uttering a sound because I knew we were already doomed. Only one of us got out of there in less than six months, and that was because her parents went broke.

I was totally silent during my first visit with my personal psychiatrist on the fifth day. He informed me that my reluctance to cooperate was detrimental to the psychoanalytical process. I responded to this by snoring as loud as possible, pretending to be asleep throughout the rest of the session. Then I was escorted back to my cell where i waited a mere four hours for dinner. These were exciting times. All I could think of was trying to find a way to break out. I knew that if I ran away and was arrested, they would just send me back to the funny-farm no matter what I did. After all, I was nuts, right?

During the third week of my confinement, the doctors took all the patients outside for a long walk on the grounds. It was a bizarre sensation to breath fresh air after being locked up in an air-conditioned environment for so long. It was the middle of summer. The plants and flowers were in full bloom. Birds flew overhead, reminding me of how tied down I was. When we went back to the ward, the doctors forgot to lock the doors behind us as they were distracted by a girl having an epileptic seizure. I took this opportunity to discreetly slip out, climbing a fifteen-foot brick wall to escape the courtyard. I ran across the cemetery adjacent to the Menninger property. The wind outside was extremely strong, and at times I thought it might knock me off my feet. Then I saw the ominous funnel cloud on the horizon, a killer tornado heading in my direction. I couldn't believe my eyes, for I had never actually seen a tornado, much less one of this magnitude. It was absolutely gigantic, tearing up the whole countryside in its path. I started to run in the opposite direction, of course.

I had never known the true meaning of fear before this moment. A tree was ripped out of the ground, roots and all, right before my eyes. I remembered *The Wizard of Oz*, when Dorothy was on the run from a tornado in Kansas. It was awfully scary, indeed, and I might not have survived if it weren't for a person in an apartment who called out to me and invited me into his home until after the storm had passed. He thought I was crazy, running around in such bad weather. He offered me a beer while we watched the tornado pass, fading into the distance. He turned on his television, and the news reported that the twister had, in fact, touched down on the Menninger grounds. The power was out there now. Also, three people were dead so far as a result of this terrible storm. I should have checked the weather forecast before deciding to run. It continued to rain for the next twenty-four hours. But I left this friendly person's house long before that so as not to wear out my welcome. He gave me another beer and I told him that I had just broken out of the hospital. He said he had a few friends that were locked up there, and that they seemed totally sane in his opinion. He told me not to give in to the powers that be, and to keep on being myself instead of going through life as a robot like most people. We parted company that night happy that we had met each other. From there, my destination was Chicago, my home town. I tried to hitchhike, but the weather was so bad that nobody even attempted to drive anywhere. Kansas was like a wasteland that night. Where could I go with no money, no transportation, and no home?

As much as I hated to admit it to myself, I was a lost soul. There was no place for me now except back at the institution. I felt humiliated, but I turned myself in voluntarily at about 3 A.M. I tried to forget about everything else and simply enjoy being in a warm bed. I was convinced, however, that there was no hope for me. A light at the end of the tunnel could not be seen. I resigned myself to endure this situation by making things very difficult for everyone around me. Given any chance to raise hell, I would do so immediately. And the next time I ran away, it would not be in the middle of the apocalypse. The memory of being chased by that tornado still haunts me today. I've had many dreams about it since then. It seems more like something out of a movie rather than a part of my real life. Actually, my whole life has been pretty unbelievable. I often find it hard to talk about myself with others whom I do not know well because they frequently accuse me of lying about things, even though it's all true.

The other patients on my unit started to like me after a while. I always told obnoxious jokes, also poking fun at the authorities to entertain myself and keep from getting bored. I enjoyed starting food fights in the cafeteria, especially if I managed to hit one of the doctors with a pie or something of the like, at which time they would call out the goons who would force me back to my cell. On one occasion I was so worked up with energy and anger that it took seven men to bring me under control.

Before smoking it all up, I shared my leftover hash with a kid named Jude. His background was much the same as mine so we had a lot in common. We developed a close friendship which lasted a long time. He joined in when I caused trouble on the ward, mostly because this was the only means of having any fun there. Consequently, he too found himself locked up there for years, but he never held it against me. I had never encouraged him to go along with my antics.

We had three pretty teenage girls on the ward at that time, until the one who had tried to kill herself with the broken bottle was transferred to the state hospital nearby. The remaining two girls were named Tara and Natalie, and both of them began to get very friendly with me during my fourth week at Menninger's.

Natalie was a local girl from Topeka. She looked like a young model with a bright future. She was tall and slender with small breasts, a beautiful face which seemed innocent, yet quite sad. She told me things that she never related to the doctors, like the fact that her father molested her sexually. She had never experienced a normal relationship with a boy.

On the other hand, Tara was a streetwise girl who had been around during her short life. She ended up in the mental hospital for running away from home and refusing to go to school, just like me. Her old boyfriend in Dayton belonged to a motorcycle gang. He used to fuck her brains out, or so she said, and now she was going through penis withdrawals. We sometimes kissed and fondled each other when nobody was watching us. I was instantly attracted to her huge bustline. I enjoyed massaging her breasts while she sat on my lap squirming back and forth. One night, with her permission, I snuck into her room. She was nude under the covers of her bed, but I was caught by the goons before we had a chance to go all the way. They hauled me back to my room, locking the door so they would not have to keep such a close eye on her. I knew eventually Tara and I would make love together.

The real angel among us was Andy, the guy who blew away his family. He acted like a perfect specimen of humanity all the time, trying to fool the doctors into thinking he was cured. He really was a pretty nice guy. Some called him "the nicest boy in Kansas." He was lucky to have been found not guilty by reason of insanity, otherwise he might be facing capital punishment because judges were now prosecuting juveniles to the full extent of the law in serious cases. As it came out in group meetings, he was an abused child who one day could not take it anymore, so his mind snapped. He lashed out violently, destroying his family. He claimed that he would have shot himself too if only he had not run out of bullets. His father was hit five times. He seemed to me like a harmless individual. Human nature is unpredictable, though. Under pressure, he could very well explode again. But the doctors were impressed with his act. They firmly believed that he would never kill again. Within a year, he was released to a halfway house, and today he is a free man.

One day in a group meeting Tara pointed out that they had heard everyone's life story except for mine. Who was I and how did I get there? Everyone wanted to hear me speak honestly for the first time. Tara moved her chair close to me and held my hand, showing everyone that she cared for me. I decided to open up and tell them about myself. First, however, I kissed Tara and slid my tongue deep into her mouth while the others watched.

I said to Tara, "I wish we could get out of here and be alone together. We should be having fun instead of wasting time here."

"Yes, but what about your life story?" she asked. "I want to hear it so I'll know more about you."

One of the lady doctors interjected, "We've been waiting for weeks to hear you say something constructive instead of acting like a Looney Tunes cartoon all of the time."

I took a deep breath and let out a long sigh. "My life story? Alright, damn it. Here it is..."

Chapter Two

It is hard finding a place to start when my whole life has been such a crazy string of events from the beginning to the present. I was born in Warren, Pennsylvania on September 21st, 1961. My sister was born five years before me when my mother was only eighteen. My father originally wanted to be an actor, but the responsibility of family kept him from actively pursuing that goal. After getting out of the service, he went to college for six years, earning a Master's degree and a chance to teach at Ohio State University. We moved to Athens, Ohio in 1966, at a time when there were political riots on campus nearly every day. The national guard was called in on several occasions to deal with the situation.

We lived in a large house on the outskirts of town, up in the hills where things were quiet. On holidays like Thanksgiving or Christmas, we went back to Pennsylvania to visit my grandparents. I remember we had huge family gatherings back then, but now most of those people are dead. My early childhood was fairly normal, I guess. I do have some happy memories, like playing poker with John Henry Timmis II, and winning twenty dollars. He probably let me win on purpose just to be a nice guy. He was an honest man who made his living by starting his own gas station at the location of a nearby lighthouse, which later became a landmark. He died of lung cancer in 1967.

We received the bad news that he was dying while we were on holiday in Europe for three months. We saw Paris and London, the Alps, Germany, everything, and it was a very good time until we heard of my grandfather's terminal illness. The news arrived by telegram, and my father cried like I had never seen him cry at any other time. This was my first acquaintance with death. I really did not understand what was happening. Lung cancer was not yet part of my vocabulary.

Perhaps my father did not even realize how serious the problem was because he procrastinated making his plans for returning home. He probably figured that we could stay a few more weeks and that his father would still be alive when we arrived home. Such was not the case. Another telegram came from my grandmother, informing us that the man was dead, so we never saw him again. That's when I realized what death really meant. He was gone forever. He could not come back. It was final and very tragic. We all cried for a whole day about it. My sister and I continued crying long after our parents stopped. Finally, my father lost control and took us to his hotel room where he punished us by whipping us with his belt. Of course, this made us cry more, the sound of which appeared to be driving him mad. At last he realized the futility of what he was doing and stopped hitting us. Unfortunately, my sister was bruised since he used the buckle end of the belt on her. Our vacation ended on a note of sadness that marked the beginning of the end for my family. Things were never really the same when we went home again. The trouble had just begun.

My father left first to attend the funeral while my mother, sister, and I stayed in Europe for a few more weeks. My father had to fly home, whereas we took an ocean liner called "The United States," which was the largest passenger ship in the world at that time. It was also the fastest, taking five days to cross the Atlantic to New York City. We met John Carradine on that trip. He just happened to be a passenger too. I remembered that he was in a number of monster movies. My sister was absolutely thrilled to see him there. I'm quite sure she got his autograph, and he gave her a great big kiss. He seemed a lot nicer in person than he did in his films, that's for sure.

On this voyage my mother met a man with whom she spent a lot of time, leaving my sister and I in our cabin. I started to get very bored, but I was looking forward to being home again. Traveling constantly for three months was exhausting. I was tired and depressed.

Back in Athens, Ohio, my parents proceeded to fight all the time about anything and everything. My mother became a real bitch who was never satisfied. Meanwhile, my father heated up the arguments by getting increasingly violent. As far as I could see, he was unsatisfied too, because he was not getting what he wanted in the bedroom. Years later he told me that my mother was the worst "lay" he'd ever had, and that she was completely repulsed by oral sex, which was his favorite activity. Whatever the reason, my home became unbearable.

One time when they were yelling and screaming at each other, he pushed her down the stairs into the basement, dragged her into his workshop where he kept all his tools, and tied her up. He started up one of his electric saws, yelling "I'm gonna cut your head off, bitch!"

My mother screamed in terror. I ran outside and around the house to the back door of the basement, thinking maybe I could get in and somehow save her before he killed her. I opened the door an inch at first, and peeked in to see what was going on. My father kicked the door shut on my nose. It hurt badly with blood dripping down onto the ground. I realized I was helpless to do anything to stop this madness, so I just walked off into the woods, sat down on a log, and cried. Later, I went back to the house. My parents acted like nothing had happened. No further mention of the incident was ever made, until now at Menninger's.

My father ignored me from then on, yet he still vented some of his aggression on my sister, probably just because she was a girl. He was developing a hatred toward women because he could not live without them. As a sexual being, he was a slave to love.

About the only times I ever saw him were at dinner or if The Beatles were making another appearance on the *Ed Sullivan Show*. He would always watch them with me. He thought they were much more talented than Elvis Presley was, and he really enjoyed their performances, especially the early ones when the group played live instead of on prerecorded promotional videotapes. My sister, however, preferred The Monkees, which was a poor TV imitation of The Beatles inspired by *A Hard Day's Night* and *Help*, two musical films starring the superior Beatles. One time my sister started a fight because both The Monkees and The Beatles were on TV at the same time on different channels. Fortunately, my dad being a Beatles fan, he ended the argument by sending my sister off to bed for the night.

Out of the blue at the beginning of 1968, my mother came into my bedroom late one night and declared that we were leaving, or running away from home to get away from my father. We left everything behind save for our clothes. It was awfully disorienting. I knew I would miss my father, and that he was not entirely to blame for our problems. My sister was glad to be getting out of there, though. Little did she know that the future would be even worse.

My mother had our escape planned well, enlisting the help of my father's best friend to fly us out of town on his private plane. Needless to say, they weren't best friends after that. This man, Al, took us to Erie, Pennsylvania where we were met at the airport by my grandparents on my mother's side of the family.

When we arrived at my grandparents' house outside of Allentown, it became obvious that they had been expecting us for some time. They had already added on an extra wing of their house for us to stay in. My mother got a job in the cafeteria at the local elementary school, so I saw her there every day. The country teachers liked to hit children on their knuckles with rulers whenever they would misbehave. Before long, my knuckles were black and blue. I was starting to develop my rebellious personality because I loathed and despised everything that was going on around me. Besides, I really enjoyed being the class clown, making everybody laugh. But the teachers told me the kids were laughing *at* me, not with me. I didn't care. All I wanted was attention. I would do anything to disrupt the normality in the lives of the people I came in contact with. My life was so abnormal that to sit quietly in class like a regular kid was totally impossible for me to do.

It was around this time that a man named Edward Killiam mysteriously came into my life. He was my mother's new lover, whom she said she had met at a florist convention in State College. He brought expensive gifts for everyone, like he was trying to buy our acceptance of him. My grandparents were extremely impressed though, especially when they found out that he owned two publishing companies worth millions of dollars. Still, I believe he actually met my mother when we were coming back from Europe without my father. Naturally, neither of them would ever admit to it.

With his financial assistance, we got our own apartment in State College while he tangled with the problem of divorcing his first wife, dumping three of his own children in the process. In situations like this, it is always the kids who get hurt the most, especially if court custody cases go on for a long time as they did in my case.

My father attempted to fight to win back his children. He ultimately lost the case when it came out during the divorce that he abused his wife, and that he was a bad influence on us. Also, he was up against big money and big-time lawyers from Chicago where Edward lived and worked. Meanwhile, my mother and grandmother went to my father's house in Ohio escorted by two police officers, and they confiscated "half" of everything as my old man stood helplessly watching them carry everything out to a moving van driven by my uncle Butch. This was unnecessary because my mother's future husband was rich. He could afford to buy her anything she wanted. But my mother wanted to get her revenge and hurt my father as much as possible. Her vengeful spirit persisted for many years after that. I often found myself caught in the middle like a pawn in a chess game. If my father failed to make his alimony payments, he would be denied the opportunity to visit with me and my sister. Yet his little payments were only a drop in the bucket compared with the immense wealth of Edward Killiam. Under the circumstances, seeing as how Edward was so well off, they should have left my father alone. Any profit they realized was easily consumed by court costs. They just did it to hurt my father. They even sent my old man a bill for two dollars' worth of cough medicine for me. I could not believe how cheap they were until my father showed me all the receipts he had saved. They hit him up for everything, including items like toothpaste, tampax for my sister, clothes, etc. Of course, any doctor bills also came his way, and when the psychiatrists moved in for the kill like vultures, those bills amounted into, literally, more than a million dollars.

Working at Ohio University, my father had a pretty good insurance plan which covered eighty percent of the damages. The rest he covered with his own cash. This left him with about a hundred and twenty dollars to spend on himself each month. It cost six thousand a month just to cover the basic expense of my term at Menninger's. But I'm getting ahead of myself with the story...

In 1969, Edward's divorce came through. We moved with him to a house in Northbrook, Illinois, a suburb of Chicago. It was like a town full of robots with everybody doing the same things: work, school, backyard barbecues on weekends, and perhaps an extramarital affair or two. A song called "Pleasant Valley Sunday" was on the radio back then. It was a satiric put-down of suburban existence, and the first tune by The Monkees that I really liked. They got better after they stopped copying The Beatles. Their song mirrored our lives, and I was happy to see that I was not the only person who thought it was all so ridiculous. I hated the hypocrisy of that time. Edward's favorite TV shows were *Leave it to Beaver* and *Dick Van Dyke*. I'm sure he wanted his new instant family to be like the families on those programs. It was a fantasy that he would never realize in reality.

I played the game for a while and went to school every day like a good boy. My mom played the Mary Tyler Moore role as best she could, frequently entertaining Edward's "sophisticated" socialite friends. It was my sister, Valerie, who first shattered the delicate menagerie. She stayed out late, cut classes at school, smoked weed, and became known as the local slut. Edward tried to beat some sense into her, like an idiot. He gained only her hatred. To her, and to me, this man was an imposter pretending to be our father. He expected us to obey and respect him, even though he had done nothing to deserve such loyalty. All he could think of to do was to call in professional help.

My sister started seeing a psychiatrist, which led her to believe there was something wrong with her, and she has suffered from low self-esteem ever since. By the beginning of 1970, she was so depressed that she just wanted to die and end it all. She voiced this desire to my mother and stepfather. They kindly responded by getting her a butcher knife from the kitchen. My mom gave it to her and said that if my sister killed herself, she would be doing us all a big favor. I watched all this from a hiding place in another room, peeping through the doorway in sheer amazement at the cold-blooded attitudes of my "parents." It was around midnight and they thought I was asleep. Who could sleep in a house where this kind of crap was going on? My sister began sobbing uncontrollably, almost like she was going into convulsions. She dropped the knife to the floor, then cried out to Edward, "I hate you, you fucking asshole!" He slapped her with his backhand, and his ring caught Valerie's face, causing an ugly bruise which was proof of the fact that we were abused children.

Before I started telling my story to the people at Menninger's, I never actually realized that I was an abused child. When life is like this every day, you start to think that everyone is living the same way. Parents do have to discipline their children, right? Even my grandmother on my father's side of the family, the sweetest lady I've ever known. "Grandma Doll," as she liked us to call her, used to keep a big wooden paddle in her attic which she would use to beat me and my sister if we began to misbehave while we were at her house.

Back to where I left off with the story, though.... Valerie asked if she could go back to Ohio to live with my father. Even though they had fought for custody of her, Edward and my mom now jumped at the chance to get rid of her. They acted very mean as they packed up her bags swiftly, setting them by the front door before even calling my father first to see if this was okay. They did not care. Valerie talked to our dad, and when he saw how unhappy she was, he agreed to take her back. He may have felt that in the end he had won the battle for at least one of his kids. He could not, as a good father, refuse to take my sister back, so he demonstrated his willingness to try to make up for whatever wrong he did in the past. My sister was back in Ohio the next day. Now I was an only child with the attention of my "parents" focused squarely on me. It was more attention than even I wanted.

They were just waiting for me to do something wrong so the

trouble would start up again. They subconsciously needed the distraction of constant turmoil because without it their lives were empty. Also, they were probably looking for a way to get rid of me, even though they would not admit this to themselves. I often found myself in the care of babysitters or surrogate families while my mother and Edward traveled all over the world. Sure enough, I started acting up in school again, getting in trouble all the time for disrupting classes. This seems to me like normal behavior for someone in my position. I really had not yet done anything which would lead my parents to believe that I was dishonest. But they did not trust me, and this fact came out in a very unfortunate way.

When they were out of town, on the day they were supposed to return, I went to a movie called *The Andromeda Strain*, then went home to meet them as planned at ten o'clock. As I approached the house, I saw that the street was crowded with police cars. Their flashing lights penetrated the night sky, casting an ominous glow over everything. I thought maybe Edward had died of a heart attack or something. I ran into the house to find both Edward and my mother alive and well in the living room talking to the police. The house had been broken into by burglars. Things were vandalized, thrown all over the place, and every drawer had been dumped out onto the floor. A search for missing items showed that the burglars had taken my movie camera, my cassette recorder, thirty of my albums, and several of my books, plus my stash of marijuana, but I wasn't about to tell the police about that. It seemed strange that everything stolen was mine.

One of the officers asked me, "Where were you tonight, boy? It's kind of late for a kid your age to be out."

"I was at the public library with a friend to see a movie," I replied with a touch of defiance in my voice. "What difference does it make, man?"

Edward said, "Sit down, John. I want to talk to you."

"What about?"

My mother cut in. "You did this, didn't you, John?"

"What?" I gasped in disbelief. "Why would I break into my own house and steal my own things? That's insane!"

Edward went on. "You did it to get the insurance money. You think you're so smart. Well, you're not going to get it, not a penny."

One of the police officers said, "Insurance fraud is an old con game. Who did you think you were fooling, kid?"

I jumped to my feet and shouted, "You got this crazy idea from these *pigs* here! I didn't do it, damn it!"

"Watch your mouth," Edward warned me.

"Why? What are you gonna do? Hit me? Well, go ahead. Show these cops what an asshole you really are."

The officers packed up their fingerprinting gear, then left hastily after getting Edward to sign some documents. On the way out, one of them wished Edward good luck in dealing with his problem: me. When Edward closed the front door I saw hatred in his eyes. I wasn't his son, but he had to put up with me.

He said, "The only way you can redeem yourself in my eyes is to tell the truth."

"I didn't do it, Edward. I didn't even know you could make money by stealing your own stuff and getting insurance money."

"Go to your room," my mother ordered me. "Get out of my sight."

I answered with a set of words I had been waiting a long time to say to them: "Fuck you."

At that point, my stepfather exploded with anger. His face turned red as the blood rushed into his head, and the veins on the sides of his neck stuck way out like they were about to burst. I thought he'd gone mad. He screamed and lunged towards me, beating me to the floor, hitting me again and again as my mother stood there and watched without lifting a finger to help me.

"You son of a bitch!" he yelled in my face, calling his own wife a bitch. "Don't you ever talk to me like that again or I'll turn you into a bloody pulp! Now, go to your room and leave us alone!"

From that moment on I hated this man with a passion, a deep emotion that gnawed at my soul all the time. The only way I could get relief was to make his life as miserable as possible, and make him regret that he had ever married my mother. For all I knew, he was responsible for the breakup of my family, for I am sure they never divulged the truth about when and where they met. In retrospect, it seems clear that there was an immediate change when we came back from Europe. Suddenly, we went from a happy family to a disaster area. And Edward was waiting in the wings with all of his money, luring my mother away with the promise of a better life.

It was not until 1987 that I stumbled upon the first solid piece of evidence to support my theory of why our family broke up. I am positive now that it was all planned out in advance.

The important point at this part of my story, though, is to show how my problems really escalated because of the distrustful atmosphere at home. I was already being punished for being a rotten kid, even though I had not yet done anything wrong. However, in the future I was determined to live up to my parents' image of me. I became like a teenage Frankenstein, turning our lives into even more of a nightmare. I wanted them to be as unhappy as I was. The day my stepfather threatened to leave us, I felt like I was really accomplishing something. But he never had the balls to walk out like he should have. Instead, he let his temper flare, and he even tried to strangle me once because I informed him that if he killed himself he would be doing everybody a big favor. Gee, I wonder where I got that line from...

I gave them what they expected. The situation just snowballed out of control due to a chain reaction of events that took place over a long period of time. When you're in the middle of it, you don't want to stop and think. You just act on impulse. I felt like I had to run away from home. It was the only way out, and maybe, just maybe, my mother and stepfather would miss me. Perhaps they would take a look at the madness they had created, realizing that much of what they were doing was wrong.

No such luck.

Chapter Three

In 1972, I ran away for the first time with a friend of mine from school. We hitchhiked up to Lake Geneva, Wisconsin, a resort area where Edward had taken my mother and I on holidays. It was a nice place, and it felt good to be there on my own. My friend and I had about a hundred dollars between us. We managed to stretch this small amount of cash so that it lasted us a pretty long time.

We slept first-class at the Blueher Hotel, the most exclusive property in the area. When my parents had brought me there before, I always stole one of the room keys, pretending to have lost it. When my friend and I were there as runaways, I had the keys to seven different rooms, so at least one of them was always empty. It was a good thing too, because this was wintertime, and there was a terrible blizzard with temperatures well below zero. We probably would have froze to death if we tried to camp outdoors.

After about a week we got tired of playing pinball machines and drinking beer, so we decided to head East, perhaps to see my sister who was now living with her boyfriend in a private apartment in Athens, Ohio. She invited us to stay with her for a week so we could smoke weed and talk. After that, I did not know what we would do. But so what? We were free. We had to take a train or a bus. Hitchhiking in this weather was dangerous. As usual, I had a plan.

The Blueher had a large game arcade with twenty pinball machines. Since there was virtually no crime in Lake Geneva, they didn't even have an alarm system on the place. We broke in there after closing time and got away with four pillow cases full of quarters. This added up to over a thousand dollars. Fearful of being caught, we hired a cab to drive us all the way from Lake Geneva to Chicago's Union Station, then paid him off with sixty dollars' worth of quarters. I told him that I had just raided my piggy bank.

The next thing we did was cash in all the change at one of the big banks in downtown Chicago. Then we went to Rush Street and bought an ounce of marijuana from a black guy outside one of the striptease establishments called The Candy Store. We smoked our brains out in a nearby park before going back to the train station to buy our tickets. We had to wait there an hour for our departure, during which time the police noticed us, and they arrested us on the spot. They took us to a detention room where we were searched and questioned. They found the bag of weed and threw it in the garbage, claiming that they were doing me a favor by not charging me with possession. The money we had stolen was safely stashed in my shoe, so they did not confiscate that. But in my wallet was my birth certificate, and my friend had a few pieces of ID, too. They put our names through their computer, discovering that we were runaways from Northbrook who had been missing for two weeks. They called our parents down to the station and released us into their custody.

My mother was obviously relieved to see that I was all right. Edward remained stone-faced and assured me that I would be properly punished for what I had done. They did not know about the arcade burglary.

When I went back to school I found that my teachers wanted me to enter "special education" classes. This way, the problem of dealing with me could be passed on to somebody else. I started seeing a psychiatrist by the name of Dr. Charles Levyman in Winnetka, Illinois. His fee was $75 per session, three times a week.

He told my parents that special education was the best thing for me, and he suggested that I enroll in Washburn Junior High there in Winnetka because they supposedly had a good program for dealing with emotionally disturbed students. Really though, the program was for retards and deaf mutes, and I got stuck in there like just another mongoloid.

I wonder if anyone took the time to look back at my test scores. My intelligence was at college-graduate level in every area, including mathematics, which is definitely my worst subject. I was bored with school because they had nothing new to teach me. Smart people learn just through being alive, and they don't need a teacher. I have always been interested in the world, so knowledge just naturally came my way. In "special ed" I was grouped with a bunch of very slow learners. Therefore, the other kids at school thought I was a slow learner, too. As things turned out, I was married and settled down before any of them even got their high school diplomas. I graduated at age fifteen.

Let me go back to Dr. Levyman for a minute. I talked with him at length about everything I thought was important, but the more I talked, the more treatment he prescribed. At one time I was seeing him four times a week. He always sat behind his desk looking like George Washington with his pen and a pad of note paper. I thought he was writing down the things that I said that could be valuable to his treatment. After many months, I grabbed the note pad away from him to see what he was writing about me. All there was to be found was page after page of stick figure doodles! Not a single shred of information! For this he was soaking my real father with extortionate bills. I became disillusioned with the value of psychiatry, never again telling Dr. Levyman my true feelings about anything.

The dentist told my mother I needed braces. She and Edward got me to call my father, asking him to pay for them under the threat that I would not visit him if he did not accomodate me. What I said was written down on a piece of paper by my mother. Both she and Edward listened on the other phone extensions while I made the call. They were using me to put pressure on my father. My mother still had the taste for revenge. I felt terrible after making that phone call, and after the braces were put on my teeth I hated them so much that I tore them off with a pair of pliers. Another thousand dollars went down the drain. When I saw my father that summer he wondered where the braces were. I told him that I was put up to that call by my mother and Edward. I was sorry, desperate for his forgiveness. The last thing I wanted was for him to be mad at me, too. I feared the worst, but he just smiled and said I had nice teeth anyway, and I didn't even need braces. Then he took me out to a drive-in movie and we forgot all about it.

He asked me if I would like to come live with him now that Valerie was out of his hair. I thought that would be great since we seemed to be getting along so well. We found that we had many similar interests, especially in stage and screen productions. He assured me that he would continue his custody fight which was still dragging on even though it was costing him a small fortune.

While I was there, I made a Super 8 home movie with him. It was a fifteen-minute horror opus in which I was an astronaut trapped on a distant planet inhabited by monsters. My father played a hunchback vampire, pulling out his false teeth so they looked like fangs and stuffing a pillow up under his shirt onto his back to create a hump. He made a pretty scary monster. The scenes of him approaching the camera lens with fake blood dripping out of his mouth were particularly gruesome. When I showed the finished film to my mother back home, she was appalled by it. Ignoring my creativity, she walked out of the room saying she didn't want to see anymore. Soon afterward, she stole the only copy of the film that I had and showed it in court as an example of the fact that my father was a bad influence on me. He did look bad in this picture, to be sure. He lost the case finally, but I never got the film back. Edward told me that he destroyed it. I wish I had it to look at again today.

The fighting and constant depression made me decide to throw everything away. At the beginning of the next semester at school, I went into the special ed classroom and lit the bulletin board on fire. Then I closed and locked the door behind me when I left. The fire spread to the carpet on the floor and soon the hallways were filled with smoke. By that time I was long gone to the beach in Winnetka where I hung out the rest of the day with a group of hippies who turned me on to their excellent marijuana. I went back to school and caught my regular bus home at 3:15. My mother was waiting for me in an enraged state of mind, for she had just gotten a call from the principal. Apparently, somebody saw me leave that classroom and lock the door. Also, I had cut out on all of my classes for the day. The principal told us to come back to school right away so she could talk to me in person. I was in serious trouble because the fire caused a complete evacuation of everyone from the school, not to mention a mild panic among the students. The damage was estimated at about five hundred dollars. Deep down inside, I did not want to hurt anyone. I just wanted to get kicked out of school. My wish was granted. They expelled me.

In 1974, I went to school at a juvenile reformatory in Lake Bluff, Illinois called Lyndon Shore. They subscribed to the Positive Peer Culture formula for confronting emotional disorders. In this program, the patient is grouped with a dozen other people of the same age who have similar problems. Lyndon Shore was for boys only up to the age of eighteen. Among my peers were rapists, drug dealers, gang members, and habitual criminals. I was there 24-hours a day, sharing a room with a member of the Insane Unknowns gang from Chicago. His nickname was Lil' Capone. We became friends and eventually ran away together, at which time he showed me how to hotwire a car.

The social workers at Lyndon Shore were sadistic to the extreme. Violence was an everyday occurrence as somebody always flipped out. We could not stand having our every move probed and evaluated. We hated being told when to eat, when to sleep, when to smoke, when to go to the bathroom. If we broke any rules, we were subjected to mental torment while the workers and peers all screamed in our faces about how terrible we were. If you spoke out of turn, it was customary for one of the peers to hold his hand over your mouth. If you resisted, everyone would hold you down on the ground and spit in your face. When this happened to me, I was so mad that they could not hold me down no matter how hard they tried. Goons from another ward had to be called in as reinforcements to get me to stop fighting, and I'm no tough guy, really. When you're that angry, you find you have strength that you didn't even know was there. Yet even I could not overcome the power of fifteen determined social workers and a gang of muscular youths. I have never felt so humiliated and low as I did when they held me down, spat in my face, and screamed and yelled at me for what seemed an eternity. Why didn't they just get down to the point and piss all over me? For the first time, I seriously contemplated suicide.

Lil' Capone and I escaped from Lyndon Shore by jumping out of our second-story window, then climbing down the steep bluff to the beach of Lake Michigan. The reformatory was fenced in on all other sides, so this was the only way to go. We did it late at night under a new moon. The sky was pitch black and it was very dangerous making our way down the cliff. One wrong move could result in death. The fall was at least three hundred feet. Luckily, I'm still here to tell the story, so you know that we made it okay. We walked south on the beach for ten miles to Winnetka. A friend of mine there took us in for the night so we could get off the streets. The law was most likely combing the entire north side of Chicagoland for us.

The next day we hotwired a car and drove to South Bend, Indiana where we split up and went our separate ways. I proceeded to hitchhike all the way out to Pennsylvania to visit an old girlfriend of mine who I had met on one of my visits to my grandmother's house. Her name was Naomi, and she lived full-time in Pittsburgh, spending summers outside Allentown at her parents' cottage. She was eighteen years old, but I looked older that I actually was and she didn't think twice about going out with me. On previous occasions we had done everything with each other short of having intercourse. When she had the cottage to herself, we gave each other long massages in the nude and sucked on each other for hours. Now, I longed to be in her arms again to feel the warmth and beauty of love. My soul had been consumed by hatred for too long.

But when I arrived unexpectedly in Pittsburgh, she turned the cold shoulder on me as politely as possible, saying she was not ready for a serious relationship, and I found myself alone in a strange decadent city without any friends. I met film director George Romero in a coffee shop, which was a high point. Also, I saw the band Led Zeppelin in concert three times. Then the movie *The Song Remains the Same* came out. It was a concert documentary of Led Zeppelin filmed at Madison Square Garden. I saw that picture fifty times in Pittsburgh so that I could get off the streets without spending money on a hotel. The usher recognized me after the fourth show and he asked me why I was sitting through so many performances. He saw that I was a real Led Zeppelin fanatic, and that I could never get tired of watching this great movie, which was true. I turned the usher on to a pipeful of reefer, the he told me that his father owned the theater. His father was out of town for two weeks on business, entrusting the operation of the theater to the guy I was smoking with. I opened up and told him that I had run away from a reformatory in Illinois. He invited me to stay in the theater when it was closed as long as I behaved myself and didn't cause any trouble. I watched the movie fifty times, but when my supply of weed was gone, I thought it was time to move on because I had nothing left to offer my new-found friend.

I made money after that by hanging around X-rated bookstores, meeting perverted older men who would pay to make it with a good-looking young stud. I started to wear makeup, portraying an androgynous image of a hermaphrodite rock and roll junkie. I was offered a part in a gay movie, but I turned it down because several corpses had turned up in Pittsburgh recently. It was suspected that these were victims of a snuff film operation, and that scared the hell out of me. Snuff films are motion pictures records of people being tortured and murdered right in front of the camera, *for real.* There actually is an underground market for such sickening pornography.

I soon got sick of the disgusting perversions around me. When I was hustling on the streets one evening, a black truck driver started talking to me and he said he was from Chicago. In fact, his rig was parked at a nearby coffee shop, so he invited me to come along with him so that I could get home. I thought he was just being a nice guy. Once we were out on the highway, though, he started demanding that I give him oral sex while he was driving this huge machine. I tried to resist because he was so fat and ugly. He pulled out a switchblade knife and said he would kill me if I didn't do what he ordered. I had no choice but to start sucking on his penis. At that exact moment, we were pulled over to the side of the road by the highway patrol. One of his brake lights was out of order. When the officers saw me, they asked for some ID. I didn't have anything with my name on it. The truck driver said he picked me up in Pittsburgh where I had been hitchhiking. The police let him go, but they dragged me down to the station for further interrogation. After taking my fingerprints, they found out who I really was even though I tried to stump them by using a fake name.

You'd be surprised how sophisticated and accurate their information systems are. George Orwell's Big Brother of 1984 arrived a little earlier than the science fiction author had prophecized. The police knew everything about everybody. All people, except illegal aliens, are in the computer files from the day they are born. They trace us through our entire lives, compiling new data, watching for repeat offenders of the law. My file was growing longer and longer with each passing day. My picture was being circulated nationwide. I felt like there was nowhere to run, nowhere to hide, and my hope for the future vanished completely. The authorities were through playing around with me. They assured me that I was in big trouble now. I could not escape the long arm of the law.

They showed me a dead woman's body in the morgue. She was undergoing an autopsy. The top of her head was cut off to examine her brain. She also had multiple stab wounds in her stomach and chest. The police told me they had found her by the side of the road. She was probably a hitchhiker who met up with a homicidal maniac. It was the most grotesque thing I had ever seen in my life. The police were trying to scare me into changing my ways by exposing me to this atrocity. I remembered the truck driver with the switchblade, and realized how close I had come to being the next victim. Slowly, I was starting to think how sick this world really is. Things like this also made me think that maybe I wasn't such a bad guy after all, not compared to the monsters who kill people for some strange sexual thrill. Perhaps I was safer locked up in an institution somewhere. God knows I was getting tired of being on the run. It seemed like fun at first, like an adventure. But now I was burned out and tired.

I was held at a juvenile detention center in Mansfield, Ohio for five days until two officers handcuffed me and took me to the airport. They personally escorted me to Chicago's O'Hare Airport. I was handcuffed throughout the entire trip. The other passengers must have thought I was a dangerous criminal. In Chicago, we were met by two local officers who took custody of me. Then they shuttled me to the so-called Audy Home, a gigantic correctional facility packed with all of the city's most hardened offenders under the age of eighteen. I was, unfortunately, the only white person on my cell block. The only entertainment there was television. Just my luck: the Roots series was on every night, depicting blacks being severely abused by whites in the era of slavery. The tension mounted while we watched it. Finally, I did get in a fight with a black guy who hated white people. However, the security guards broke up this scuffle before either of us got hurt. Four weeks later I was transferred to yet another institution. It seemed like the authorities didn't know what to do with me.

It was the beginning of 1976. Jimmy Carter had just been elected. The weather in Chicago was cold, snowy, and relentlessly bad. I became a patient in the psychiatric ward on the top floor of Evanston Hospital. The doctors there told me that a judge had ordered my parents to put me away at the institution of their choice. Otherwise I was destined to be a ward of the court and they would deal very harshly with me. If I thought Lyndon Shore was bad, they warned that I would never want to see St. Joe's, the other local reformatory which was nothing more than a prison. It was suggested in no uncertain terms that I cooperate with the staff at Evanston Hospital so they could psychoanalyze me and perhaps arrange for my release *if* I could convince them that I was ready to rejoin society, to function like a normal young man of my age.

With the prospect of release hung in front of me like bait,

they conned me into being a model patient. I went to their poor excuse for a school every day and promptly did all the work that was assigned to me. I told my life story as it stood so far in group meetings. My personal psychiatrist discovered how much anger was bottled up inside me. I also did my best to help other patients on the ward cope with being locked up. By the end of eight weeks, when my review meeting came up, I was positive that they were going to set me free. I thought I'd probably go back home to my parents, who had moved to a nicer house on Private Road in Winnetka. I was ready to make a new start and put the madness of the past behind me.

The review board, with my parents there, gathered around a big table in one of the offices. As soon as I walked into the room I knew something was wrong. Edward was biting his fingernails. My mother could not look me straight in the eyes. The doctors themselves seemed nervous, too, which was odd because they never showed any emotions at all.

I sat down at the table and said, "I've been waiting for this day to come. You people better have some good news for me."

Edward replied, "We don't feel you're ready to come home yet."

I smashed the table with my fist. "What?! You mean I'm gonna have to stay here? I can't take it anymore. It's driving me sane."

"Sane?" my psychiatrist asked, smiling. "It seems you've still managed to hold on to your sense of humor."

I told him, "I can't do anything else but laugh, or else I'd start crying, and I don't wanna give my parents the satisfaction."

My mother said, "We never wanted this for you, John. You did it to yourself. You have to face the consequences of your actions."

I felt myself getting really mad at her. "It's not all my fault! It started before I was even born, man! I've been living in hell all my life thanks to you, but you purge yourself of all the guilt! Maybe you and Edward should go see a psychiatrist and think back to when my family was torn apart. I was denied a normal childhood from the beginning, just because you met Edward, the asshole with all the money!"

"That's not true," my mother insisted.

"Bullshit!" I stammered. "You dumped my father for him! You dumped my sister for him! And now, you're dumping me, too!"

My psychiatrist interrupted this argument by saying, "You will not be staying here, John. You will be going to a hospital in Topeka, Kansas called the Menninger Foundation. Our diagnosis is that you are a psychopath. We feel you need extensive treatment to cure the disorder. You will probably be there for two or three years, depending on your behavior. First, they will make their own diagnosis, and if they agree with us, then you will have to stay there until the age of eighteen, unless you can show them you are cured, in which case they might let you out sooner."

"I'm not falling for that con game again," I said in a disgusted tone of voice. "You tricked me into cooperating with you. I opened up and trusted you, telling you things I've never told anyone before. I thought you understood me. I guess psychiatry is a pretty overrated profession. If I'm a psychopath, then you could grab anyone off the street, subject them to eight weeks of interrogation which is like having your mind raped, and you could declare them to be in need of treatment. I'm not crazy."

My psychiatrist said, "We don't think you're crazy."

One of the other doctors at the table interjected, "Most psychopaths are not crazy. In fact, the vast majority of them are exceptionally intelligent individuals. But they feel no remorse when they do things that are wrong, and they will do anything to get what they want. We feel that at this time you could be a danger to yourself and others. We believe you have suicidal tendencies. Hopefully, after you receive treatment you will grow up to be a regular citizen with a decent place in society."

I mumbled, "A robot, a zombie, with a job and a wife and two kids and a little spotted dog, with a barbecue on the back porch and a mistress at one of the hotels downtown..."

Edward told me, "You have a dangerously terrible outlook on life."

"Well, I'm only a product of everything around me, man."

I went back to the ward that night, waiting for morning to arrive, at which time me and my parents would be flying down to Topeka. My probation officer warned that if I ran away, when I was caught they would send me to St. Joe's. I had been locked up for twelve weeks straight, through all the depressing holidays like Thanksgiving, Christmas, and New Year's Day. The only time I breathed any fresh air was when they transferred me from the Audy Home to Evanston Hospital.

Ironically, there was a movie on TV that evening called *The Psychopath* about a maniac on the rampage who butchers women with a pair of scissors. Everybody on the ward watched this awful picture just to pass the time. The doctors wouldn't let us watch a much better film on another channel titled *One Flew Over the Cuckoo's Nest* because it might have an adverse effect on our states of mind. Well, I was in a rotten mood anyway, thinking about being locked up in a mental hospital for the next two or three years.

I decided to become a vegetable and never cooperate with the doctors again. I had nothing to lose.

Chapter Four

The staff at Menninger's took another eight weeks out of my life preparing their diagnosis. However, that was nothing compared to how long they wanted to keep me there. I was like a goldmine to them. They agreed with Evanston that I was a psychopath, adding that I had schizophrenic overtones, and they were certain that if they released me I would be dead within a year, either by suicide, drug overdose, murder, or whatever other ways you can think of for a scumbag like me to bite the dust.

I was transferred to the Hilltop Unit, which, as you might suspect, was at the top of a hill. The patients there were all boys up to the age of eighteen. I was disappointed that they did not put me on a ward with girls, but I suspected this was due to the time I was caught sneaking into Tara's room late at night. Such things are not forgotten. They record every move you make in their log books.

I was committed to the Hilltop Unit for an unspecified amount of time. It turned out to be two and a half years. Tara was locked up on the Whitney Unit for girls, where she stayed for three years. I hardly ever saw her after that because she was always in trouble for one thing or another, and so was I. Both of us spent a lot of time in solitary confinement.

They never gave me any drugs at Menninger's. They must have known that I liked to get high, and would be using them to escape reality. Other people were getting shot up with large doses of Thorazine every day, so really I'm glad they left me alone there.

The first thing I was struck by when I came onto the Hilltop

Unit was how friendly all the patients were with each other. They were normal kids from screwed up homes with rich parents who could afford to put them away to dispose of the problem. I don't think there was anything wrong with any of us. Yet we had all been diagnosed as mentally ill, in need of clinical therapy. We just wanted to grow up too soon, that's all. Everybody there seemed at least three years older than they really were. We built up very close relationships over the years. There were usually fifteen patients on the ward. If one of us was released, a replacement would pop up immediately. Strangely enough, there wasn't one new arrival that I didn't like. And fortunately, everyone liked me right away. I still had my razor-sharp sense of humor and rebellious attitude. It was us against them, so for a while I united us all against authority, effectively creating chaos on many different occasions.

I did not want to go to their little school with babysitters posing as teachers. Instead, I took the GED test to get my high school diploma. I was told that I achieved the highest score ever in the state of Kansas at that time. This reinforced my opinion of myself, making me feel better. I was sure there was nothing the matter with my mind and that a great injustice was being done by keeping me locked up, especially after already getting my high school diploma. I should have been out banging beaver and having fun with my friends.

What I really wanted to do was start a rock and roll band. My singing voice was exceptional before I trashed it by smoking cigarettes year after year. When I was younger, one summer my parents had sent me off to the Chagoyan Theater Camp in Ozaukee Lake, Wisconsin. I had appeared in a stage version of *West Side Story* as the lead character. Leonard Bernstein played the piano as I sang great songs like "Maria" and "Tonight." He was a personal friend of the owners of the camp, and he frequently lent his assistance to their theatrical productions. Robert Mitchum came by during rehearsals, lending constructive criticism. Out of a thousand people, I had the best vocal range, spanning five octaves. Everyone admired my singing capabilities, and since then I've always wanted to be a musician.

While I was locked up at Menninger's, my parents bought me a guitar and I started writing my own songs. One of the first follows here. I later made it into a record called *In the Can*.

It's kind of hard to write a song
when I've been inside these walls so long.
I think of my best friend outside.
I wrote him a letter the other day.
It wasn't long but at least I tried.
I didn't have all that much to say.
Diamonds are falling from the sky.
I can see them through my bulletproof window.
Once in a while the storm will die.
I'd like to trip while I watch it snow.
And when I finally get out of here
I'm gonna buy me some whiskey and a case of beer.
Think of my best friend outside.
I got a letter from him today.
It wasn't long but at least he tried.
He didn't have too much to say.
I've been following the trails
but they only disappear.
I end up walking down the rails,
but they've always led me here.
I've done my time out on the street scene
with the guys who pull dirty tricks.
I've messed with the junkies and the closet queens
until I found myself needing a fix.

But it's kind of hard to write a song
when I've been inside these walls so long.
And when I finally get out of here
I'm gonna buy me some whiskey and a case of beer.

I managed to escape from Menninger's six times over the years. The first time it was easy because I talked the doctors into taking the patients out to see a movie called *Night of the Living Dead* at the university in nearby Lawrence, Kansas. The fools did not know this was the most disgusting horror movie ever made. I had seen it before, though, so I knew they would be appalled by it. There are graphic scenes of dismemberment and cannibalism as a plague of flesh-eating zombies conquers the world. While everybody was captivated by utter disbelief of what they were seeing on the screen, I snuck out one of the exit doors and ran off into the night, free at last.

I had saved my six dollars a week allowance so that I had enough to buy a Greyhound Bus ticket to St. Louis, Missouri. From there I hitchhiked to Chicago. I was lucky and got a ride with a cool hippie-type, about thirty-five years old, who had a nice stash of weed to smoke. I bought a couple of joints from him for the road, and he dropped me off on the south side of the city. I caught a CTA train up to the north side, then walked up the beach to Winnetka, avoiding the streets so as not to be caught by the police. The summer weather was very pleasant, and it seemed like consolation enough to be alive just to be able to smell the fresh air and enjoy the beauty of nature. When the sun went down, I took off all my clothes and went for a refreshing swim in the waters of Lake Michigan.

Later, I went to a friend's house in Winnetka. His name was Jake Ludlow, and I had met him when I was in special education. His two older brothers also became good friends of mine because they enjoyed partying, listening to loud music, and other activities which drove their parents up the wall. Their stepmother did not like me at all. She thought I looked like a hoodlum. Fortunately that did not have an adverse effect on our friendship. We had a lot of happy times together. I helped them build a great tree fort in their back yard which they let me sleep in sometimes. I almost broke my neck once climbing around up there while I was stoned. At that time I was consuming as much dope and booze as I could lay my hands on. I felt like I was making up for lost time.

I visited all of my other close friends from the past, too, including Jim and Larry Maxwell who lived right next door to my parents' house! Can you imagine? Here the police are combing the whole country looking for me, and I was right next door! These people had a gigantic house like a castle, and we could do anything we wanted without getting hassled by the parents who might have been on the first floor while we smoked joints up on the third floor. Phil Donahue later bought this house after the Maxwell family moved out.

The Maxwells were always very nice to me. There were seven children between the ages of fifteen and thirty. The eldest sister, Lucy, had been frequently writing to me at Menninger's. I always thought that we could be romantically involved, but she fell in love and was married by the time I got out of this mess. Her parents were quite open-minded. In fact, the reason why the kids never got into any trouble was because there weren't so many restrictions being imposed on them. For example, it was better to get high in the house than to do it outside where they could get into a hassle with the police. The atmosphere of their house was ambient and comfortable. Therefore, the kids liked being at home. They had nothing to rebel against, either. I wished my parents could have been more like the Maxwells.

The highlight of my excursion had to be when I went to

see a sweetheart from my school days named Elizabeth Swift in Northbrook. We went steady for two years before my life fell completely apart. She was a lot like me with sort of a masculine personality, though her body was mostly feminine, indeed. We shared the same contempt for authority figures, and we hated with a passion to be controlled by others. She was getting in trouble all the time now, finding herself in the same situation that I had been in a few years earlier. Elizabeth feared that her wealthy parents were going to lock her up in a mental hospital. This did eventually happen because she continued having problems after that. She, like me, was totally disobedient.

I really liked her a lot. I almost wished we could get married and settle down together. This was impossible, though. She told me she was on my side and that she loved me. We made plans to get together again soon, but I did not see her next until years later as I was arrested the next day. Such is life...

After going to a party and spending the last of my money on hashish, I went back to the beach and fell asleep. In the morning, I went to a grocery store to shoplift some food like a blithering idiot. My jacket was stuffed with goodies when I ran into my mom on my way out. She was surprised to see me to say the least. Of course, she knew I had run away from Menninger's, but she wondered how I had made it all the way "home" without getting caught. She said she wanted to talk to me for a minute, and that I should wait outside for her to finish shopping. I went out and threw the food I had stolen into the garbage, then waited impatiently for her to come out and talk. Only a minute or two had passed when a squad car pulled into the parking lot with its lights flashing. A policeman jumped out, running toward me. I tried to get away, gaining a good lead on him as I ran as fast as I could. But a good Samaritan citizen joined in the chase. He was a very big guy with huge muscles, and he was able to hold me down while the officer slapped his cuffs on my wrists. They dragged me off to the squad car where my mother was waiting.

"I'm sorry," she said with a tear in her eye. "I had to turn you in for your own good."

I told the big guy with the muscles, "I'm not a criminal. You should learn to mind your own business."

He asked, "So what did he do, anyways?"

The officer answered, "He escaped from a mental hospital. Isn't that right, Mrs. Killiam?"

My mother walked away, got into her car, and drove off.

I was taken to the Winnetka police station where they fingerprinted me, took mugshot photographs, and locked me in a cell by myself. I waited there for about twenty-four hours until the police escorted me back to Kansas on a jet plane. Again, I was handcuffed through the entire trip and the other passengers kept looking at me constantly, like they were trying to figure out what crime I had committed.

The other patients on the Hilltop Unit were visibly disappointed to see that I had been caught. But they welcomed me back and wished me better luck next time. It wouldn't be so easy to get away again though, because now the doctors confined me to my room at all times. I never saw the outside world at all for months. They weren't going to give me another chance to escape, not after the fiasco of going to see *Night of the Living Dead*.

"By the way," I asked one of the social workers, "how did you like that movie?"

"Sick, John. Really sick. It was the scariest movie I've ever seen. I don't think it was helpful to the other patients at all. We really made a mistake going on that field trip."

This was the precise reaction I had been looking for. The movie was very disturbing because it is of psychological relevence, like a parable of our society in which zombies have assumed control, and those with any humanity left are being eaten alive. After all, we've had zombies in The White House for years, right?

The doctors were nice enough to let me out of my room for one night to watch *The Midnight Special* in the TV lounge. David Bowie and his Spiders from Mars did a fantastic concert from the Marquee club in London. The act was very bizarre, androgynous to extreme, with Bowie dressed in very bizzare "gay" costumes. Glitter rock was at its height. Now stage theatrics were just as important as the music. It was a new way to create a generation gap between the flower children of the Sixties and the punks of the modern age. David Bowie was an artistic pioneer in a world where shock value was the only way to get attention. His Ziggy Stardust alien fag superstar image set the tone for the decade, and for a while people thought it was cool to be gay. Now, with the AIDS scare, all that has changed.

After seeing Bowie, I started wearing a little makeup myself: a bit of eyeliner, mascara, lipstick, face powder, and blush. I applied it carefully so it would be discreet, making me look better without having other people know I was wearing makeup. As time passed, I became more bold, laying it on a lot thicker. It bothered me that people were trapped in the traditional roles of male and female. I wanted to cross the line and create a combination of the two which was how I really felt inside.

During my stay in solitary confinement, I read a lot of books like *Valley of the Dolls* and *The Eagle Has Landed*. It was nice eating three full meals a day from the cafeteria and smoking hundreds of cigarettes. My contact with everyone in the outside world was cut off. I refused to see Dr. Petersen for my psychiatric sessions. I was consumed by a strange feeling of ennui which made me content to be a vegetable. I never became bored because I have a very active mind. I wrote a lot of new songs during that time, many of which were later made into records in the 1980's. Summer passed into winter while I waited for time to catch up with me. One day I would get out of there and live my life the way I wanted to. Until then, I had no desire to do anything at all. However, to be a zombie all the time requires dedication. Inevitably, I needed someone to talk with.

This is when Rachel Couenneoeur, one of the nurses on the ward, started coming into my room at odd hours for long conversations. She was twenty-five years old, single, a college graduate, and an employee of Menninger's for the past two years. She said she worked there because she wanted to help people like me who had been failed in every other aspect of life. If she could save one young man from destroying his life, then her whole career would have been worthwhile. I became the target of her efforts to the point of obsession. That was fine with me. I was glad to see that somebody cared about me, especially an attractive young lady like her. Before long, I found myself developing an irresistable crush on her, wondering what it would be like if we could make love together. I was sure that if I felt this way, then she must have been feeling the same way, too. I confronted her about it on Thanksgiving Day when she brought me a turkey dinner and ate with me in my room. She kept me company for hours that night, knowing how depressed I was being locked up on a holiday. I was starting to get used to it, though. If I let it bother me I probably would have driven myself crazy. Thanksgiving would have been just another day if it weren't for Rachel. She made it a special occasion, which I will always cherish.

After we finished eating the delicious food, I said, "Rachel, you've been paying an awful lot of attention to me lately. I wanna let you know that I appreciate it. I really like you. We've tried to go beyond the standard patient-doctor relationship to become friends with each other. But now I must confess that I am extremely attracted to you and I wish we could be more than just friends. I want to be your lover. Now, I suppose you will either slap my face or give me a nice kiss on the lips."

We were sitting on the floor with food all around us. She moved everything aside, put her arms around me, and gave me a wonderful kiss that made me feel very happy inside.

She told me, "I do want to be more than your friend, John. You are a unique person. I've never met anyone like you before. When I took this job, I never bargained on falling in love with a patient. It's not something I was looking for. But here you are, and it's good that now you know my true feelings. I was afraid to say anything about it until I was sure we were both experiencing the same emotions."

I laughed and held her hand tightly within my grasp. "We have quite an awkward situation here, my dear. What are we going to do about it? Couldn't you be putting your job in jeopardy if anyone else on the staff found out about this?"

She replied, "You have to keep your mouth shut about it, John. Maybe some day in the future when you get out of here we can have a relationship. It feels painful for me to want someone and not be able to have them. When I go home to my bed at night I think about you and fantasize about making love with you. It's just a dream that we can't bring into reality at this time. Love is supposed to make you feel good, but for some reason I feel like my heart is breaking inside. I hope I haven't upset you. I might be doing more harm than good."

"Don't be ridiculous, Rachel. I always find myself in improbable situations. This episode fits right in with the rest of my crazy life. You can be sure that I never thought I'd fall in love with somebody on the staff here. I'm happy that even in a clinical, cold place like this real feelings still exist. Thanks for opening up to me and telling me about your fantasies. I think about you every night in bed, too."

Rachel started rubbing my shoulders and my neck. "Would you like for me to give you a massage?"

"I'm not going to say no to that."

"Then take off your clothes and get into bed. I'll go get some moisturizing lotion and give you the best rubdown you've ever had."

Chapter Five

One day Dr. Petersen came into my room saying that it was time for me to have a physical examination, and he also wanted to take some X-rays of my head for some reason. These X-rays showed that I had a crack in my skull. How it got there I have no idea. Could this be responsible for my psychosis? They subjected me to another brainwave test, and this time I did not think about music, so it came out normal. Seemingly dumbfounded, Dr. Petersen ordered more X-rays. I became concerned about radiation, but he assured me there was nothing to worry about. It was no worse than sitting outside on a sunny day. A week later I was called back to the lab for more X-rays of my entire body. I didn't understand why. Since they were professionals I just let them get on with their work, momentarily forgetting about my vow not to cooperate with the doctors. When they asked me to go back to the X-ray lab a fourth time, I said 'enough is enough' and refused. I was suffering from extreme headaches which I feared might be caused by radiation. Dr. Petersen insisted that I was just being paranoid. Still, paranoia could be an acute perception of reality. Whatever the case, they weren't going to give me any more X-rays. If it isn't dangerous, then why does the technician have to stand behind a sheet of lead when the machine is activated?

As much as I tried to fight it, I inevitably felt the need to run away again. After being let out of solitary confinement, I was able to go with the rest of the group to the laundromat on Sundays. I packed everything I wanted to take with me into a laundry bag, conspiring with fellow patient Dan McLaughlin to run as soon as we had a chance. I thought it would be more fun to go with somebody instead of alone. That way we could give each other moral support, and keep each other from doing stupid things that could result in our capture by the police. We stayed gone for six weeks, until he turned eighteen and realized his freedom. Then we went our seperate ways.

To start out with, we only had forty dollars between us. That was enough for two bus tickets to Kansas City. After that, we hitchhiked to Dan's home town of Independence, Missouri. His parents were out of town, so we stopped by his house to raid the refrigerator and liquor cabinet. He found another thirty dollars by searching all over the place, and he called a friend to get a car ride into Illinois. Our ultimate destination was Lake Geneva, Wisconsin. Within twenty-four hours we were halfway there.

We must have been lucky because we did not get arrested trying to hitchhike the rest of the way. Somewhere out on the highway, a middle aged black guy tried to pull over onto the shoulder to pick us up. He did it so abruptly that a truck smashed into him from behind, causing extensive damage to his Pontiac, and forcing open the trunk. Both the truck and the Pontiac stopped while Dan and I chomped on our fingernails nervously. The black man jumped out of his car with blood all over his face, and he started yelling at the truck driver like a maniac. They quarreled over whose fault it was as a police car could be seen approaching from the distance.

"Let's get out of here, John," Dan said, pulling on my arm.

"Wait a minute."

The popped trunk on the Pontiac revealed a big ziplock plastic bag filled with pharmaceutical pills, thousands of them! I quickly grabbed the bag and we ran off, hopping over a fence to get off the expressway. Seconds later the police arrived at the scene of the accident. We may have stolen the poor guy's drugs, but we saved him from being arrested for them, so we didn't feel too bad about it. Besides, he was already too intoxicated or he wouldn't have caused that accident.

This unexpected turn of events was worth a lot of money to us when we got to Chicago. We had Valium, Quaaludes, codeine, White Cross speed tablets, and other various assorted drugs that sold quickly at three rock concerts we attended. People literally ate them up. We made over a thousand dollars in just three days, plus we traded for LSD and marijuana. We still had hundreds of pills left, too!

The bands we saw were Gentle Giant, Billy Joel, City Boy, Lake, Nektar, and Alice Cooper. One of the shows had three bands on the same bill, lasting more than six hours. It was a lot of fun, especially when we beheld the onstage theatrics of Alice Cooper, who made David Bowie look like Bozo the Clown. He was ten times more outrageous with his mascara smeared all over his face and a ten foot snake wrapped around his body. He sang angrily about many things like institutionalization in his "Ballad of Dwight Fry." Meanwhile, he rolled around in broken glass, vomited, hung himself, electrocuted himself by pouring whiskey on his microphone... He cut his wrists and chopped up a stage hand with a sword, then topped it all off by being decapitated with a guillotine. The production was top notch, and it all looked real to me. I've been an Alice Cooper fan ever since.

Unfortunately, after all of the concerts, fights broke out in the streets at the intersection of Broadway and Lawrence where the theaters were located. Heads were cracked and people were arrested, but Dan and I always managed to slip out without incident.

We took the Milwaukee Road train from Union Station up to Lake Geneva. I didn't have the keys to the Blueher Hotel anymore, but there was a nearby condominium development called Blueher Springs, which was not yet completed. We stayed in an empty unit on weekends when the place was full of people from Chicago, and then broke into their condos during the week when the place was empty. We didn't steal anything. We just raided their refrigerators and liquor cabinets, then left everything just as we had found it so the tenants would never even know we had been there. Surely they would not notice a missing TV dinner, a bottle of whiskey, or a couple of pills from the medicine cabinet, as if we didn't have enough. We were able to go back to the same condominiums many times because nobody even knew intruders were there while they were gone. Most tenants were rich residents of Chicago who brought their families to Lake Geneva on weekends, and the rest of the time their cottages were unused. If they ever read this book they'll probably freak out.

Okay, I was out of control. I admit it. But I have been punished for whatever wrong I did when I was younger, and all this madness ended in 1978 when I was finally released by the Menninger Foundation. I went on to get married and work for the Chicago Police Lodge #7 for a decade, never getting into trouble again once I had the freedom I craved. That explained, let me get back to where I left off with the story.

Just for kicks, we did lift a Polaroid camera and some film, and Dan took nude pictures of me laying on top of a table with drugs all around me as I held a knife to my throat. We sent the pictures to Rachel Couenneoeur at Menninger's. I also wrote a short letter to her saying that I was sorry if I made her worry about me, but I couldn't stand being caged like a wild animal anymore.

Of course, I was sealing my own fate, condemning myself to further time at the institution if I was caught. I felt like I had nothing to lose though, since I believed they were going to hold me there as long as they could, anyway. My self-destructive qualities really began to emerge at this point. My brain was soaked with dope and booze to the point that I became an entirely different person.

When Dan turned eighteen, we celebrated by taking LSD and going back to Chicago, but not before robbing the reliable pinball machines in the arcade at the Blueher. Now we had about two thousand dollars because we made off with four pillow cases full of quarters. It took a few days to cash them all in for bills, and we saw another concert at the Aragon Ballroom: Black Sabbath. Then we parted company. He took a Greyhound bus back to Independence, Missouri and started a new life. I couldn't wait until that day came for me. I was still only sixteen years old!

Now alone, I wasn't sure what to do. I had to make it on my own. We had split up the money, so I had around a thousand bucks on me. First I went to Northbrook to see a pizza delivery man from Roselinni's Restaurant who doubled as a marijuana dealer. I had known him for years, and he used to pretend like he was making pizza deliveries to my house when he was, in fact, selling me reefer, which he had discreetly packaged in an innocent-looking brown square box with a menu stapled on top. Unfortunately, he doesn't work there anymore, but he was there in 1977 when I went back to Northbrook.

I tried to contact Elizabeth Swift, but she was locked up in some asylum out East. It seemed a shame that she had to go through the same routine as me. She was such a sweet girl who just wanted to have fun. Her strict parents had her labeled as a problem child from the start. We lost contact with each other for a long, long time.

I became involved with the Chicago gay underground by calling up my old hairdresser from Winnetka, Miguel Fuldano. He lived in a high-rise apartment on Lake Shore Drive with his roommate Tommy Kurtis, one of the city's most notorious and beautiful drag queens. Before I went there, I visited a boutique on Howard Street to buy some new clothes so I would look sharp. Along with a black leather motorcycle jacket, I got a pair of tall black boots like the ones the Nazis used to wear. Once I put on some makeup I looked totally bizarre, like a perfect hermaphroditic lover just waiting to be deflowered. We smoked weed and popped pills and engaged in a homosexual orgy that lasted through the night, ending with them squirting their sperm all over my face. I didn't know why, but I loved every second of it. My female side was taking over. Maybe I really did have a dual personality. The people at Menninger's could have been right when they said I was partially schizophrenic.

The next day I felt ashamed of myself for what I had done. No matter how much it turned me on at the time, it still didn't seem right for men to have sex together. I wanted to be with a woman, but I did not lose my virginity until several months later when I was on my next runaway excursion from the institution.

Before leaving Chicago, I was talked into attending the 1977 transvestite beauty contest held at a gay bar which no longer exists. Tommy Kurtis won top honors that night, strutting his stuff down the aisle just like Miss America. It dawned on me then that faggots love women so much so that they actually want to be women themselves. Transvestitism was a tribute to femininity, and imitation is the sincerest form of flattery.

At the transvestite beauty contest I met a heavyset man from Winnetka named Gordon Moore, whose daughter I went to school with a few years back. He told me he had a friend in Las Vegas who produced gay sex movies for big money, and that if I ever wanted a job I should call him and he would hook me up. Though I had turned down a similar offer in the past, the proposition now seemed quite lucrative to me. The gay crowd appreciated me and complimented me, making me feel like something really special, but all they really wanted to do was fuck me in the ass, both literally and figuratively.

Gordon took me to dinner at Barnaby's in Northbrook while he told me about how he had been involved with the gay community for years, even though he had a wife and children as a front to cover his secret lifestyle. He was a respected citizen of Winnetka, owner of a store which specialized in interior decorating. His wallet was as fat as he was, and I knew I could make a fortune from him if I wanted to. He said he also knew a lot of other people who would be willing to pay as much as $200 an hour to have sex with me. One such individual was the manager of the restaurant where we were eating, a man by the name of John Gacy. Gordon said he'd be happy to introduce me to him if I wanted to make some quick money. Luckily, my financial situation was pretty good, so I turned down the offer. Instead, I wanted to learn more about Gordon's Las Vegas X-rated film connection. Gordon gave me his business card and told me if I was really interested I should call him some time in the near future. He knew nothing of the fact that I was a fugitive from the law.

For those of you who don't know, it was discovered in 1979 that John Gacy murdered thirty-two young men from the Chicago area, and he buried their bodies in the crawlspace underneath his house. Most of the victims were young men who had charged him money for homosexual relations. They were tortured for many hours before they died. Gacy now sits on Death Row awaiting his execution.

I don't know what it was exactly, but my instincts told me I was getting in over my head, especially when Gordon said the guy in Vegas might like to keep me as his personal sex slave at all times for payment of $10,000 a month, with services most likely being rendered first. These men did not appreciate the beauty of androgyny, nor did they have any beauty to offer. All they had was the lure of money, and they resented always having to pay just to get somebody to touch them. I decided it would be best for me to just get the hell out of town as soon as possible.

I called up my mother on a payphone to let her know I was alright. She told me the police were hot on my trail through Missouri, Illinois, and Wisconsin. I had been charged with a burglary at the Blueher, and if they caught me I would be going to St. Joe's for sure this time. It looked like the only way out for me was to make my way back to Kansas and turn myself in at the Menninger Foundation without getting arrested first. That meant I had to stay off the highways. I couldn't hitchhike this time. My mother offered to meet me somewhere, but after the last escapade with her I said "No, thanks."

At the end of the conversation I told her not to worry about me, then hung up the phone without informing her of my decision to go back to the hospital. I wanted it to be an unexpected surprise with impact and shock value. Nobody, especially the patients, would believe that I was actually turning myself in. I represented a freedom fighter to a lot of people. We had a mad rash of runaways at Menninger's over the next year, a few of which were extremely clever in their means of escape. It became harder and harder as the rules were stiffened, but where there's a will, there's a way.

Well, if I was going to go back, I at least had to live it up a little more, so I traveled first class on a jet airliner from Chicago's O'Hare Airport to Topeka, drinking massive amounts of complimentary booze on the way there. Then I took a cab to the local Holiday Inn where I stayed for the night and ate a big breakfast. I was exhausted, coming down with a bad cold in my throat which permanently changed my voice. Ever since then I've spoken in a lower tone than anyone else I've ever met. This resulted in the loss of at least one octave in my singing range, too. But it added character to my vocals which came out on the records I made in the future, like I had been to hell and back and loved it. I no longer sounded like a teenager.

One of my favorite musicians at that time was Lou Reed,

formerly of the Velvet Underground and singer of the underground classic "Walk on the Wild Side." I was surprised to see an advertisement in the newspaper for a concert he was doing in Lawrence, Kansas, just about twenty-five miles away. Lou Reed was appearing on a double bill with a punk rock group called Ian Dury and the Blockheads. I went to see the show, giving away free pills to anyone who wanted them just so I could get rid of them. Afterwards, I still had so many hundreds left that I had to throw them away, but not in a garbage can. I left them on a bus hoping someone else would find them who could do something with them. They were worth a lot of money.

Lou Reed was very upset that night because the sound system was malfunctioning, causing a lot of feedback. He smashed microphones and cursed at his stagehands, performing a mere forty minutes before he walked off the stage. He left behind an audience that was just as angry as he was. Most people left the theater right away when the house lights came on, but a few of his most hardcore fans like me stayed behind and moved into the front rows. We cheered and called out the titles of Lou's old songs like "Heroin" while a couple of confused law enforcement officers stood by watching. They probably could not understand why we kept shouting "heroin." Surely they had no idea it was the name of a tune. After a half hour of this they told us it was time to go home. Then Lou Reed came back onstage. As if to make up for what had happened earlier, he played for another whole hour, covering the best songs from his solo career like "Coney Island Baby" and "Satellite of Love." When he left the stage for the second time, everyone was certain that the concert was over. There were only about thirty people left in the audience now. I remarked that Lou had not played any Velvet Underground material. We all started screaming enthusiastically once again for "Heroin," his fifteen minute anthem to junkiedom. Sure enough, after a long break he came back and played for another whole hour! What started out as the worst concert I had ever seen turned into one of the best. He performed all of the songs we wanted to hear, putting his whole broken heart into the streetwise lyrics like the Lenny Bruce of rock and roll.

I became heavily influenced by his style: the deadpan monotone of his voice taking an unflinching look at the dark side of life. This was entertainment for adults. The music industry had grown up, and Lou Reed was a sign of that maturity. Today he is considered by many to be the Godfather of Punk, a new wave which conquered the world when disco finally died. Lou was no stranger to glitter rock either, as David Bowie and Andy Warhol were producers of his best recordings. I enjoyed it so much because he was completely different from the commercial garbage on the radio. His lyrics portrayed the world as it really is, not like the fantasy we think it should be. Therefore, Lou Reed remains an important artist whose work will stand the test of time. When today's disposable rock stars are long forgotten, his name will live on thanks to his "cult" of fans who continually spread the word about him. If you ever see him in concert, be sure to leave your bubblegum and fraternity jacket outside the door. Otherwise, you might get your ass kicked.

All right, enough of my tribute to Lou Reed. After the show, I was lucky enough to get a lift back to Topeka with a guy named Ken who had been sitting next to me in the theater for the last four hours. He took me to his house where we smoked a few joints, and then we went out to a bar. Many beers later, he had to leave to meet his girlfriend. I stayed at the bar, enjoying what I knew would be my last alcoholic beverages for quite some time. I called Menninger's and talked to Rachel. She said she had received my letter containing the weird pictures of me. I told her that I would be turning myself in later that night. She was surprised to hear I was in Topeka. I thought this might be a good opportunity for us to get together outside of Menninger's, but my cold was getting so severe that sex was the furthest thing from my mind. I really felt terrible, worse than ever before. So I sat around the bar into the late hours of the night trying to kill the germs with straight whiskey and beer. It didn't work, though. I succeeded only in getting totally smashed.

It was about two in the morning when I took a bus from the center of town down Sixth Street, past the state hospital to where Menninger's was located. I remembered the pills I had left in my pocket, and in a drunken stupor I just left them there on the bus. I stumbled up to the Hilltop Unit feeling like I was ready to vomit. It caught me off-guard when Rachel came outside after I rang the doorbell. I did not expect to see her at that hour, but she had waited for me.

"Wow, John, you look really cooked," was her first reaction.

"Thanks. I can use all the compliments I can get."

She stepped outside onto the front steps and gave me a quick kiss, then looked around to make sure nobody was watching.

"Where did you get the leather jacket?" she asked.

"Chicago, the Windy City. Damn, it's cold up there."

"What made you decide to come back?"

"I can't run forever. The police would have busted me sooner or later. Besides, I did enough heavy partying to hold me over for a while."

She said, "Judging from those pictures, I'd say you went over the edge. I was worried about you."

"Did you show those photos to anyone else, Rachel?"

"Just one of them. You were naked in most of them, so I couldn't show those to anybody. Where in God's name did you get all those pills?"

"It's a long story. I'll tell you about it later, okay? Right now I just want to go to bed and crash out for about two weeks like a vegetable. I do still have a bed here, don't I?"

"Yeah, John, but not in the same room. They're going to put you in solitary confinement in an empty room with nothing but a bed. They don't even want you to have your guitar because they think you might try to hang yourself with the strings or something. If you're good maybe they'll bring you some books to read."

"And how long do I have to put up with this shit?"

"Probably a month or so, until you gain the trust of the staff. Are you sure you want to come back?"

"What choice have I got, unless you and me run away together?"

"I don't want to destroy my life too, John. Life is hard enough as it is. Well, are you ready to go back to the ward?"

"Ready as I'll ever be," I said sarcastically.

Chapter six

My mother and Edward came to Kansas for group therapy sessions in the spring of 1977. These meetings included Dr. Petersen, Roy Suvino, who was the unit manager, plus a social worker named Carol Anne, my parents, and myself. Edward spent most of the time grinding me into the dirt over all the terrible things I had done. Meanwhile, my mother filled the ashtray with cigarette butts.

Dr. Petersen said, "John, you have been under our care for a long time now, but we find it impossible to help since you refuse to cooperate with us."

"I never wanted your help," I snapped at him. "You can't help somebody who doesn't want help, no matter how screwed up you think they are. So what's the point?"

"We can keep you under lock and key," he answered.

"Can you? You haven't been having much luck so far."

Carol Anne told me, "You won't find it too easy to get out of solitary confinement. We're not going to let you out until we're sure you have changed."

"Into what?" I implored. "What do you people want to change me into? I can't pretend to be someone I'm not."

Petersen replied, "We just want to see you lead a normal life."

"Then let me out of here right now! That's the way to end this madness! I'm going to fight against you for as long as you hold me against my will!"

"That's not a very constructive attitude," my mom cleverly interjected. "Why can't you try to build a more positive frame of mind?"

Edward shook his head back and forth in disgust. "He's a rotten kid. He's always been bad, from the very beginning."

I spat on his shoes. "That's what you expected, so that's what you got."

My mom told me, "We never lost our hope for you, John. We always believed that in your heart you never really wanted to hurt anyone, except maybe yourself, subconsciously."

I stood up from my chair, pacing the conference room, feeling claustrophobic. "Will you shut up with the textbook psychology crap? Before you know it these clowns will have you thinking I'm a homosexual because I secretly want to go to bed with you. Freud was insane, in case you're not aware! You can take his books, and Karl Menninger's books, and all the other crappy books you've been reading and stick them right up your ass, which is where your brains are anyway! You can't learn how psychology works in the real world just by reading about it! And no matter how much you do learn, it won't do you any good until you can master your own existence! Before you pass judgement on me, why don't you look at yourselves, all of you? You're not perfect. You're not even good. You just know how to lie and hide behind the hypocrisy of our society with its bullshit institutions, morals, and religions. How many of you can actually say that you are happy with your lives?"

Edward said, "I'm content and happy with my life, John."

"Then you're the most cold-blooded, narrow-minded, self-centered bastard I've ever met in my life! Let me out of here! This fucking meeting is over! I'm not talking anymore!"

Roy Suvino grabbed ahold of my arm. "Sit down and relax, John."

"Get your hands off me, man! You can't make me do anything

I don't want to do! Haven't you figured that out yet?"

My mother seemed disappointed. "So, that's it? Don't you have anything nice to say to us?"

"No. Don't you have anything good to tell me?"

"Well, I do have something to tell you, John, but it's not very good. Your sister, Valerie, has been confined to a mental hospital in Pennsylvania. She overdosed on drugs and had to have her stomach pumped. The doctors think she may have attempted suicide. She's in the state hospital because your father is too cheap to pay for better care like Edward is doing with you."

I had returned to my chair and was smoking a cigarette, dragging on it heavily. "Who are you trying to kid? My father is paying the Menninger bills with his insurance policy."

"The insurance doesn't cover it all," Edward informed me.

"You have insurance, too, don't you? How much does it cover?"

Edward answered, "Roughly fifty percent after the deductible."

"Well, I know for a fact that my father's insurance with Ohio University covers more than fifty percent, so you should be getting refunds in the mail. I wouldn't be surprised if you figured out how to make money out of keeping me here."

"That's absurd!" my mother stammered. "Where do you get ideas like that? You're just like your father."

"Maybe that's why you have such a problem with me. I'm a lot like him as far as my personality is concerned. And Edward, to you I must represent the seed of your wife's first lover, so you hate me deep down inside even though you might not even admit it to yourself."

Edward sat there shaking his head again. "You think you're so damned smart. You've got it all figured out, don't you? You know more than these specialists who've had years of training, right?"

"I didn't say that. But I know more about *us* than they do."

Carol Anne tried to change the subject. "Let's go back to

something you said earlier, John. You said you were a homosexual. Are you?"

"I didn't say that, either, but... okay, sure! I'm a homosexual!"

My mother asked, "How long have you been wearing mascara?"

"Ever since I got into glitter rock and realized that I have a female side as well as a male side."

Edward chuckled and rolled his eyes at me.

Carol Anne said, "Since we've met, John, I have been studying androgyny and I have an interesting book on the subject which you might like to read. It even discusses the impact of David Bowie on the modern fashions of our society in this decade. I do not believe you are a homosexual. I think you are attracted to an image of fantasy portrayed in the stage theatrics of today's rock stars. You have frequently expressed your desire to play music professionally when you get out of here. You know that you are very good-looking and makeup can be used to make you look even better. Also, this is a new way for you to be different from everybody else. No, I don't think this has anything to do with homosexuality at all, even though you may have had some gay relationships in the past."

"Miguel," my mother mumbled under her breath.

I explained, "Miguel is a gay hairdresser from the most exclusive salon in Chicago's North Shore area. My mother was kind enough to introduce me to him back in 1974 when I needed a haircut. How did you know about us?"

She said, "I only suspected. God, now I'm sure."

"Listen to me, Mom. Don't you dare call the police on him. I know that it was illegal for us to be together since I'm a minor, but he didn't force me to do anything. As a matter of fact, I'm the one who initiated it by approaching him. I like him."

Dr. Petersen attempted to ease the situation. "Everything said in these meetings is confidential and will never leave this room."

"Oh, really? Then why are you taking notes of everything we

say? Or are you just making stick figure doodles on that pad of paper?"

Carol Anne interrupted with more of her philosophy. "When you had sex with this man, you must have approached him out of sheer curiosity. This is completely natural and it is nothing to feel ashamed or guilty about. Most boys and girls experiment at a young age before losing their virginity to a member of the opposite sex. When you meet the right girl and fall in love, you will be heterosexual for the rest of your life, most likely. Believe me, you won't have any trouble attracting desirable ladies. Women today are tired of the standard macho stereotype of men with big muscles who sit around drinking beer and watching sporting events on TV. Intelligence is what really turns women on today, and you definitely have plenty of that."

"Thanks for the compliments. I guess you're not as dumb as I thought. Except for a few minor details, you've managed to see through a lot of the bullshit and figure out the way I think on this subject. It is sad, however, that I've already met the right girl for me, but I can't do anything about it because I'm locked up in this place."

"Who is she?" asked Roy Suvino.

"I can't tell you. I promised her I would keep it a secret."

Dr. Petersen winked at me without anyone else noticing, and I got the impression that somehow he already knew about Rachel.

He stood up from his chair, saying, "That's all the time we have for today, but we have another scheduled meeting at two o'clock tomorrow. I assume I'll be seeing you all at that time."

I told everyone, "I don't want to participate in these meetings with my mom and Edward anymore. We're talking about some very private matters here which don't concern them in any way. Personally, I don't think it's any of their business what my sexual preferences are. That is unrelated to the reasons why I am here.

In just this one hour-long session I've already said way too much, even though I vowed to fight you at every turn. If you want answers to some of your unsolved questions, maybe you should get my real father to come down here."

Petersen said, "We've written to him to see if he would participate in your therapy. Unfortunately, he did not respond."

My mother looked upset. "What about tomorrow's meeting, then? Do you want us to just go home and forget about it?"

"Yeah. Forget it. I'm sorry. Just forget it."

Carol Anne suggested that they stay in town as planned. That way, at least they could have private sessions with her to discuss things we may have skipped over. I did not even say goodbye to my parents when Dr. Petersen escorted me down the long hallway into the front lounge of the Caulder Building where we sat down and talked for a short time.

He said, "John, you represent a very interesting case to me. Not only that, but I like you as an individual. Something happened to you in your past that made you the way you are today. You can turn that into a positive thing with your high level of intelligence. We have learned a lot about you since you have been here. Yet, I think we could go deeper and find out things you have forgotten. I'd like to try to hypnotize you. Would you go along with that?"

"I don't think I trust you enough for that, Dr. Petersen."

"Well, I'll have to work on that, and we can discuss it again at a later date, alright?"

My mother and Edward walked by, accompanied by Carol Anne and Roy Suvino. They stopped at the front door, waiting for me to acknowledge their departure. I went over to them and tried to be more polite.

"I guess I'll see you in a few months," I smiled. "One of these days all this will be behind us. Then maybe you can stop being my parents and become my friends."

My heart was not in what I was saying, but I knew these would be the last words they heard from me for a long time, so I wanted to say something halfway positive. This way they wouldn't always feel as bad as they did when our group therapy session ended.

My mother kissed me on the cheek. "Are you sure you won't change your mind about the meeting for tomorrow? I think we're making progress."

"I can't handle it. My decision is final."

Edward shook my hand. "At least you speak your mind truthfully. That's always gotten you into a lot of trouble, but it's probably the thing I admire most about you."

"I didn't know you admired anything about me."

"Hang in there, John. You're going to come out of this okay in the end. Good luck. Take care of yourself, and please don't run away again. The staff here is on your side."

When they were gone, Roy took me back to the Hilltop Unit for another exciting evening in solitary confinement. Currently, I was reading *Tales of Power* by Carlos Casteneda. I would read twelve other books besides that one before they let me out of my otherwise empty room again.

All of the patients on the ward had nicknames bestowed upon them by their fellow inmates. There was Crab, Runt, Okie, Sea Bisquit, Egg, Slim, and others I can't remember. The name they gave me was 'Veg'. That was an accurate description of me at the time because it seemed like I never did anything. Basically, I just waited for the doctors to let me out of solitary. It took about five weeks for this to happen, but even then I was still locked inside the ward and could not escape. After all that time had passed, though, it was nice to just be able to watch TV and talk with the other guys. A few of them played guitar, so we frequently sat in the hallways having jam sessions. I showed them a few tricks for playing rock and roll by utilizing shortcuts not demonstrated in music books.

Everybody was being very rebellious at the time, causing a lot of problems for the staff. I had to refrain from getting involved or they would just throw me back in my room again and take away all my possessions. The other patients probably thought I'd be happy to join them in a mass revolt and breakout which they were planning. Rob Guillory pointed out that all the doors were made out of wood so it would be possible to break through them in sheer numbers if they could get enough people to go for it. He said if I didn't go with them, I'd be the only patient who stayed behind. If such was the case, they really didn't need my added strength. Surely fourteen powerful young men could kick down three wooden doors and deal with the two security guards on duty late at night. I was always independent too, not wanting to go along with the crowd, so now I was being well-behaved just to be different. That was a switch.

Out of the whole bunch, only two were still at large the morning after the breakout. Most of them were arrested on the streets within a few hours. I wondered if now the whole unit would be in solitary except for me. This did not happen. At the next group meeting, Rob Guillory apologized for orchestrating the escape plan, explaining that he had done it because he wanted to get out and see his girlfriend from the Whitney Unit who had also run away. Everyone expressed their need for contact with girls. They promised to control themselves in the future and that such an episode would never happen again. Unbelievably, none of them were punished in any way. I felt cheated after all the time I spent in solitary, yet I could not be mad at them for not having to go through the same thing. They were lucky that the doctors were receptive and understanding.

Jason Shippy and Darrel Todd Johnson, the two who were not caught right away, stayed gone for three weeks. They stole a car and drove across America on a wild sightseeing trip. The law caught up with them somewhere in Arizona. When they came back to Menninger's they were put in solitary for a couple of weeks. Then things went back to normal. All of the patients went back to school and carried on with the usual routine. My school days were over, though, so I was left alone on the unit during the day Monday through Friday. These were the hours Rachel Couenneoeur was on duty. I was glad to have her all to myself.

I usually stayed up all night and slept most of the day, seemingly living up to my nickname, Veg. My odd hours caused me to miss a lot of meals in the cafeteria, and I lost a considerable amount of weight. I was six feet tall. At one time I was down to a hundred and thirty-five pounds. This happened when I got food poisoning from some lukewarm chili they were serving for dinner one night. Other patients got sick from it too, so they never gave us chili again after that, thank God.

Rachel woke me up every day when she came to work by pulling down my sheets and giving me exquisite massages with moisturizing lotion. I always slept in the nude. Her skilled hands caressed me everywhere. She took her time doing it, as if she was enjoying it as much as me. No woman since then has ever been able to make me feel that good. While she rubbed me I listened to her talk about her life, her dreams, and ambitions. Her ultimate goal was to someday move to Alaska, to get as far away from everything as humanly possible. She wanted to live a life of solitude and quiet security in a log cabin of her own construction. She liked nature, wide open spaces, snow, and fresh air. It sounded great to me. Did this fantasy existence include a man, though?

"I don't think I'll ever meet the right man," she answered.

"What about me, Rachel? Don't I fit the bill anymore? You said that you were in love with me."

"I still am. But who knows how much longer you'll be here? It could be two years. Will you even feel the same about me by then?"

"My feelings will never change no matter how much time passes or how far apart we are. That is the meaning of true love, isn't it?"

"Yes, John. It's too bad we had to meet here under such extremely difficult circumstances."

I said, "If we wouldn't have met here, then we never would have met at all. I'm glad at least one good thing came out of my being locked up at Menninger's. I still don't think I belong here, really. If they would just let me go, then the police would never hear from me again. Growing up in a mental institution is for crazy people, right?"

"Since you've been here, John, I've seen you filled with pain, anger, and hate. It's hard for me to witness that day after day because of the way I feel about you. If it will help put your mind at ease, let me say this: nobody is to blame and everybody is to blame."

"What? I don't dig it."

"Society itself is responsible for your dilemma. It imposed the standards by which we live. Your parents did what they thought was right for you based on ethical principles of how to raise a family. This code of ethics or rulebook was not written by them. They followed the guidelines their parents gave them, and they followed the professional advice of everyone around them. If you hold this against them, it will be a weight on your shoulders for the rest of your life. The thing about revenge is that you never get enough."

I was impressed by her eloquence, but my attitude did not change. Was society responsible for the fact that my sister and I were abused as children? Was society to blame for my father beating up on my mother? How did society arrange the breakup of my family and introduce Edward so conveniently? Why was my sister also locked up in an institution if none of these things had any relevance?

Almost stumped, Rachel thought for a while about all of these questions. For the first time she asked me for a cigarette, even though she did not smoke. She only took a couple of puffs without inhaling, then put it out. It tasted terrible because we had to roll our own cigarettes with cheap tobacco in tin drums. Patients only received six dollars a week as an allowance, and that had to go a long way. A drum of tobacco with rolling papers cost about three dollars and would last for three weeks.

She eventually started talking again. "It is possible that your father was an abused child, or he may have witnessed his father abusing his mother. I'm willing to bet your family has a long history of this sort of thing. People don't just act like that out of the blue. They learn their behavior from adults before they are even able to talk as children. If your mother met Edward while she was still married, she was looking for a way out and he provided it for her. In the broad sense, everything can be traced to something before it, and everything can be blamed on society."

"You're a smart lady, Rachel, and you have a way of putting things which does help me reconcile all the facts in my brain. Your views are not unrealistic or even optimistic. While we don't always agree on everything, you're not full of shit like most of the people who work here, so I respect your opinions. When we talk I feel like we are really opening important new doors for the first time, like we're really accomplishing something and going somewhere. Too bad you're not the unit manager so you could sign my release papers and I could get the hell out of here. What is it about me that made you decide to let me into your heart like this? Tell me. I want to know.

"The first thing I noticed about you, John, was your eyes. You have the bluest eyes in the world, like the clear sky on a sunny day. And your face... It could be a pretty girl's face, but it's yours. When you are clean-shaven, you look like a prince. I knew there had to be a brilliant mind lurking behind that lovely face so I watched you very closely and saw you live up to all of my expectations. You are the most stubborn person I've met, which can be an admirable quality if it's used in the right way. Anyone else would have given up the fight long ago. I just hope that when you get out of here it doesn't become a struggle within yourself. One day you won't be fighting against the whole world, but your soul might still be in turmoil unless you can relieve your anger somehow. When the time comes you will have to mature beyond the level most people can achieve. If you do, you won't have to fight to prove that you're right because you won't need to be forgiven. Then you can move on to get just what you want out of life, and you'll finally be a happy person."

Chapter seven

Time was starting to lose all meaning for me and I lost track of it completely. Every day was the same and I welcomed any change. I was particularly bored on days when Rachel was not scheduled to come in. Dr. Petersen tried to gain my trust by visiting me more often. He understood that I did not want to have any more psychiatric counseling, but there were other ways he thought he could help me. He still wanted to hypnotize me. First, though, he told me about his past success with hypnotism and that it was very useful for finding out information locked deep in the past, or memories so painful that they had been blocked out. Many childhood trauma cases remained unsolved until hypnotism was employed.

Also, he used to do LSD experimentation back in the Sixties when the hallucinogenic drug was legal. He thought it was a great tool for exploring the subconscious mind while still awake. Having taken LSD myself on at least twenty different occasions, I knew exactly what he was talking about and the subject interested me very much. While Dr. Petersen could no longer legally administer LSD, he claimed that he could reinduce the high because the drug never leaves the brain even after it has worn off. His procedure was called "guided imagery" and it consisted of bringing the patient back to a semi-hypnotic state while guiding him with gentle words on a trip through some sort of fantasyland to the sounds of electronic music. A flashback could be brought about if the patient had the ability to recognize it and drift along without being frightened back into reality.

Another thing Petersen had been involved with was telekinesis, in which people were actually able to move objects with the power of the mind. He claimed that he once saw a roomful of twenty people levitating in mid-air at a scientific research convention back in, yes, you guessed it, those fabulous Sixties. I deduced that he must have been stoned from the LSD experiments when he saw this. My humor was not appreciated. He took the subject very seriously and asked me to believe him. After all, he was a doctor at the country's most respected psychiatric institution. He also said he once saw a girl bend a fork using only the power of her mind, and an Indian who stuck a coathanger wire through his arm but felt no pain. I laughed and said that anyone who would stick a coathanger through his arm had to be out of his mind, perhaps so crazy that he could just ignore the pain.

Again, Petersen seemed offended by the fact that I would not believe him. It did seem pretty incredible to me. My interest in him had been aroused, though. I agreed to let him try to hypnotize me and take me on a guided imagery trip. He took me off the Hilltop Unit to his office where I made myself comfortable by lying down on his couch while he tried to put me under his spell with a swinging pendulum. After an hour of effort, he was convinced that I was too stubborn to be hypnotized. Something inside me would never permit me to be put completely under by the control of another person. In my head I was afraid he might program me to become a different person, to do things I would never do. He could have made me into a robot, and I would not have known it because when a person wakes up from hypnotism they cannot remember what was said and done while they were in that altered state. I told him this, and now he became intimidated, like he couldn't understand why I didn't trust him.

"John, do you think they would let a mad doctor work here at

Menninger's? I'm in this business to help people, not to create an army of zombies who will do my bidding. Youv'e seen too many horror movies. But even if you were with a doctor that you trusted, I still think it would be impossible to hypnotize you. Something in your past is being blocked out and your mind has built up a defense mechanism to protect it. The memory is still there, if only we could get to it. We might have better luck with guided imagery because that way you will still be the one in control. Lie back on the couch again and close your eyes."

I did this and he moved his chair right next to the couch so he could massage my head, concentrating on the temples on each side. This was where he said the LSD information was stored. I had a headache, but it quickly went away. After a few minutes he put on a record album by Brian Eno called *No Pussyfooting*, one of the strangest records ever released on the commercial market. Each side featured one continuous piece of music played through an electronic synthesizer. There were no lyrics, and it set the perfect mood tone for an adventure into the realm of expanded consciousness.

Petersen started to speak softly, but clearly. "Imagine that the doors are open and you can go anywhere you want. Where would you be, John? Where would you be?"

"I've always wanted to see Paris again, but Philadelphia will do."

"Come on. Be serious."

"Alright. I'm in the Bahamas, man."

"Yes, and you're walking alone on the beach at sunset. Try to picture it in your mind. Listen to the ocean waves as they break on the sand. Smell the salt in the air and feel the heat of the sun."

I told him I was having a hard time keeping my eyes closed, so he gave me a sleep mask which covered only the eyes and held them shut. Then I could relax those muscles along with all the other ones in my body. I pictured the beach with the palm trees and the water and birds flying overhead, casting their shadows onto the sand. I thought of beautiful nude women sunbathing and rubbing tanning oil into their flesh. As my mind wandered I felt like I was starting to fall asleep. Abstract thoughts that were totally out of context started flashing through my head. Suddenly, my body jumped in a violent convulsion which lasted only a split second. Petersen must have noticed this, but he did not say anything about it. Instead he continued to guide me on a tour of the inside of my brain.

He said, "You walk away from the beach now and follow a path through the trees, kicking coconuts out of your way as you go. The path is a long one leading up a very steep hill to a cliff overlooking the ocean. You are confronted there by a wizard dressed in a colorful costume. He offers you a peyote button, then waves his magic wand and disappears. At that moment, a total eclipse of the sun occurs. You look straight into it even though it is so bright that it hurts your eyes. When you can take it no more, you finally wander back down the path in a daze with sunspots in your eyes. Now you are on your own to experience whatever kind of trip you want to experience. Drift away by yourself into the deepest caverns of your mind."

I was hovering in a state somewhere between sleep and being awake. The abstract images flashed by more rapidly and frequently now, like they were being shown to me by someone else and I had no control over them. I saw a decapitated woman's head lying on a floor. I saw an image of my Grandma Doll pointing a pistol at me and pulling the trigger. I also witnessed flashes of a skeleton in a chair with a lampshade on top of its skull, dinosaurs destroying a Protestant church, and a man in a gas mask with a syringe reaching out to me. These were like pictures in a slide projector being revealed at irregular intervals. The first continuous, moving "hallucination" I experienced was of me trapped in a whirlpool of murky waters, spinning around and around and being sucked down slowly into the vortex. I remembered that this used to be my most terrifying recurring nightmare when I was a child. Fear swelled up inside of me. In my dreams I always woke up before I was sucked through the center of the whirlpool. Now I wondered what would happen if I had the courage to go through the vortex and see what was waiting for me there. Perhaps I would discover what the meaning of this nightmare was. As soon as I consciously made the decision to stick with it, I felt like all the blood in my body was rushing to my head, and I was engulfed by the murky waters. My "vision" was blinded by brilliant light. Next I saw what appeared to be the negative of a photograph showing a sewer drain in the street with a hand reaching up out of it!

"John, wake up. Can you hear me? John?"

"Yeah. What? Oh, are we finished?"

"The music ended. It's been over an hour. Tell me about what happened. I could see that you were in an altered state."

After I told Dr. Petersen about my experience, he was surprised at how much information he had to work with. I really was an easy subject for guided imagery, perhaps because the last time I took LSD was not very long before that. Aside from the scary parts at the end, I thought it was a fantastic legal high and I hoped we would be able to summon up more flashbacks in the near future. It never worked like that again, however, no matter how many times we tried it.

Dr. Petersen's remarks regarding the first guided imagery trip were as follows: "I believe that you really want to find out what is at the root of your problems. Life is like the Domino Principle in action. The way you react to things has a direct relationship to what has happened to you in the past. Your mind attempted to go back as far as it could by recalling that forgotten childhood nightmare. The decapitated woman's head on the floor obviously represents your mother, especially in light of the story you once told us about how your father tied up your mother in the basement workshop and threated to cut off her head with an electric saw. The image of being shot by your grandmother symbolizes your distrust of the entire family. I think the skeleton in the chair was you, and the lampshade on top of your skull could mean that you felt like a piece of furniture in your home. The dinosaurs destroying the church, in my opinion, represent your contempt for religion and its morals, and you probably fantasized that your family was trapped inside being killed while you stood outside and watched. The fact that you were able to specify that it was a Protestant church lends credence to my hypothesis since this is the religion of your family. The man in the gas mask with the syringe could have been me or just a distorted stereotype of all the doctors who have been treating you. The most significant portion of your trip was when you descended into the whirlpool, and the very next thing you saw was the sewer opening with the hand reaching out of it. This was a warning to yourself, John, that your life is going down the drain. There was probably more to it than that, but we've made a great start in uncovering some of your subconscious thoughts. We'll try again sometime next week to see what else we can learn."

But as I said earlier, we were never again successful in conjuring up LSD flashbacks, although guided imagery still was an interesting and often enjoyable, relaxing diversion. I began to like Dr. Petersen's company more as time went on because he had finally gained my respect. I was impressed with his analysis, and I liked to hear about the work he had done in the past, especially his early associations with Timothy Leary and Ken Kesey, two pioneers in the field of LSD experimentation before the courts outlawed the drug. Still, I never did believe his story about the roomful of people levitating. Whenever the subject came up, I always used to joke with him about it, saying with tongue in cheek that he must have been stoned when he witnessed this phenomenon.

I think it was in the month of May when Rachel gave me the bad news that she was quitting her job on the Hilltop Unit for a position at Southard School, which was Menninger's year-round learning facility. On the morning of her last day she brought breakfast to my room and then gave me another one of her invigorating massages. I decided it was time for me to return the favor, so she bravely took off her shirt and let me rub her even though one of the doctors could have walked in at any moment. I had learned a lot from her about how to rub someone the right way, so I knew that she really enjoyed it.

After that, I took a quick shower and got ready to go outside with her, for she had received permission from Dr. Petersen to take me to the zoo. This was a real treat for me since I had not been out for more than a minute between offices during the last three months. I did not pay much attention to the animals while we were there. My thoughts were focused solely on her. The weather was nice and the grass was green, and we ate a picnic lunch on one of the park benches. All that was missing was a bottle of wine.

That night, although she was already off-duty, she stayed with me. We went out again when another social worker named May Vandross came to work. The two of them had the audacity to take me and four other patients to an erotic film festival at the University theater in Lawrence. We all acted like perfect gentlemen, enjoying the program immensely, but we kept ourselves from becoming too aroused. Rachel and I sat next to each other feeling the heat, yet all we could do was hold hands because the others were watching us very closely.

When the show was over we all had dinner at a local pizza parlor in Lawrence before driving the short way back to Topeka in the van. Everything was paid for by the Hilltop expense account.

I was touched by the fact that they were trying to show us a good time and doing things outside the acceptable norms of the institution. I was taught the right way to have sex by watching those films, for they were all tastefully done without degradation of the female as in other pictures I had seen. They also demonstrated how to implement birth control without any contraceptives by always having the man pull out at the moment of ejaculation. Pornography is a great educational tool.

This fine day came to a close around eleven o'clock. Rachel took the van keys back to the office, then came to my room to say goodbye. I started to feel nervous and upset, and for the first time she saw a tear come out of one of my eyes. That caused her to cry more emotionally so that her whole face turned red. We put our arms around each other, hugging tightly, and her tears dripped onto my shoulder. Embarrassed, we both regained our composure quickly.

"So this is it, eh?" I asked.

"No, John. I'll still be working for the Menninger Foundation, so you can see me any time you want to. This doesn't have to be the end of our relationship. I'm moving into a house nearby with Elaine Nance," who was the secretary at Hillside. "I'll give you my phone number as soon as we have it connected, but I'll be over at the school five days a week. You can always reach me there until then. You could have been in my class if you didn't already have your diploma."

I shook my head and smiled in a twisted way. "You wanna talk about having a crush on the teacher? That would have been too much. The situation we have here is odd enough. What made you decide to make this move? It seems like it came up suddenly, and it's going to take me a long time to get used to your not being here. Why are you leaving?"

"Well, the pay is a little better. I need the money. I've been trying to work my way into that position ever since I came here. Plus, it is pretty hard to work here on Hilltop now that I've fallen in love with you. My feelings keep growing stronger as we come to know each other better. I can't concentrate on my job anymore, and I'm not being much help to the other patients. Dr. Petersen and I had a long talk about this. You don't represent a patient to me now. You're the one I love. But a social worker has to be objective in order to be effective. Do you understand where I'm coming from?"

"Yeah. I'm just sorry to see you go. I won't look forward to waking up in the morning tomorrow."

I held her tight once more, and for the first time I slid my long tongue down her throat when I kissed her, wiggling it back and forth inside her mouth. Then I reached down with both hands to grab her ass. I had to bend way over to do this because Rachel was just over five feet tall. She pressed her crotch against mine firmly.

"One day we're gonna make love like we always wanted to do," I said.

Rachel replied, "I'm sure I'll never meet anyone else like you. No matter what happens, I'll always feel the same. I promise not to be a stranger. Goodbye, John."

When she was gone, I suddenly felt a powerful surge of depression setting in along with a high level of anxiety. There were only two things for me to do, either sit around and cry about my impossible situation or write a new song about it. I chose the latter, creating a song called "The Gift of Love," the lyrics of which expressed all of my emotions for Rachel. It was never made into a record, but I did perform this number in the 1985 concert movie *Cosmic Lightening*.

I've been living on the edge of insanity,
fighting all of humanity,

but I never quite broke down
until you came around
because you made me come out of my shell,
and now you know me very well.
You're the only person I've ever really cared about
and, so help me God, I'll never shut you out.
Sometimes when I talk to you
the words that I say fall apart.
But you understand my meaning
because these words come straight from my heart.
And now that I have the power
to carry on with life
I'll be living in my own little world
wishing you were my wife
because I love you. Only you.
If you will be my lover
until the end of time,
then I won't ever feel bad
when I lose my mind.
I know that you're feeling the same,
so let me ease our pains.
Hold onto me until I am you
and you are deep inside me.
You are, oh, so beautiful
that you've captivated my eyes.
But I know you'll look different when we make love.
You'll look even prettier!
Can you hear what I'm saying?
You could make me the happiest man.
I wanna make you the happiest woman
in any way that I can,
because I love you. Only you.

Baby, baby, don't forget me!
Baby, baby, don't reject me!
Don't let it end before it starts!
Baby, baby, I need you now!
Baby, baby, we can make it somehow!
Baby, baby, give me one more chance!
Baby, baby, let's make romance!
Let me into your heart!

The lyrics to this song were published in an anthology of poetry by the patients at Menninger's, and everyone wondered who was the object of my desires. Turning to another page in the book, however, revealed the answer to that question, for Rachel also published a poem (she was the only staff member to do so), and she dedicated it to me.

Since she was no longer working on Hilltop, Rachel must not have felt that she had to keep her love for me a secret any longer. In fact, she told Dr. Petersen about it so he could help her deal with her feelings. Eventually word filtered through the entire institution, and for a while the rumors about me being a faggot subsided. Still, it was a sad and hopeless situation because we could not fulfill our need to make love with each other. I continued to fantasize about her for a while, but things were never really the same even though Rachel was still employed by Menninger's. As time passed, I saw less and less of her until I finally just had to put her out of my mind and forget about her.

Chapter eight

The Menninger Foundation could not or would not release me. Dr. Petersen said he thought they were doing me a favor by keeping me from going "home" to such a terrible atmosphere where they were sure I would self-destruct. I did not understand why they could not just let me get my own apartment somewhere, perhaps even in Topeka, and let me live on my own. I might have been more willing to cooperate with them as an outpatient. As it was, it did not take long for me to start getting the itch to run away again. Since I was already being punished, I felt like I might as well do something to deserve it. If I did get arrested and sent to St. Joe's, then so be it. I was going to test those threats and see if they would actually back them up, thus destroying my life. If they did, then the entire juvenile reform system was a joke.

My old friend from the Hillside Unit, Tara Baldwin, devised her escape by calling a friend of hers and asking this friend to phone in an anonymous bomb threat to the institution. When the patients were evacuated, she took this opportunity to run off through the cemetery when the staff was looking the other way. Two girls from the Whitney Unit also seized on the opportunity, taking a momentary leave of absence from which they did not return until being arrested about a week later.

Rachel's replacement on Hilltop was a sexy-looking young lady named Olivia who was working her way through college to get a degree in psychology. Part of her education required her to work part time at Menninger's for eight weeks. She did not last that long.

I quickly achieved her friendship and trust, and I convinced her that my being locked up was a mistake. Then I totally bullshitted her by telling her that I was falling in love with her. She fell for the bait, saying she felt the same way about me, and she helped to plan my escape, even loaning me some money because I was broke. I knew that in the end this would probably ruin her career, but I did not care. I was just using her to get what I wanted, and she paid the price.

One day when she was leaving and the door to the cafeteria was already open, she left the second door unlocked. All I had to do then was get by an old lady at the reception desk. Once outside, there was a security patrol car in the area, so I ran the other way and climbed a high fence to get to the highway. There was a lot of traffic that day. I almost got hit by a pickup truck when I hastily crossed the pavement. On the other side I had to climb another fence to get to a baseball field and recreational park where I sat down in a crowd of sports fans who were watching a game featuring two minor league teams from Kansas. After I caught my breath for a few minutes, I went to a phone and called Olivia, my accomplice.

"Hello?"

"It's John. I'm out. I think the security guard saw me climb the fence to the highway, so I better not walk the streets. They're probably looking for me already. I got past the receptionist without being seen, though. Anyways, I better stay here. How long will it take for you to come pick me up?"

"I can be there in fifteen minutes, okay?"

"Great. I'll be waiting, and Olivia, thanks a lot. I really appreciate this."

That night, I went to her house in downtown Topeka where I had the pleasure of meeting her friends: a bunch of drug-crazed junkies who had an outrageous amount of heroin and needles spread out on the kitchen table. The house was filled with marijuana smoke, and the beer and whiskey were flowing freely, too. The people all seemed like hippies, leftover relics from the Sixties. Olivia eagerly sat down at the table and tied up her arm with an electrical cord while some guy jabbed a needle in her arm, shooting the dope directly into her veins. When the injection was complete she untied the cord, letting the blood flow through the rest of her body. Her eyes rolled up into the back of her head and a big smile came across her face.

"You want a poke, John?" she asked, slumping into her chair.

"No, thanks. I don't shoot heroin. But if you'd be nice enough to let me snort some through my nose I'd really like it."

"That's cool, man," said the guy who was doing the honors with the needles. Get me something flat and clean to cut it up on."

With some effort, Olivia reached into her purse and pulled out a little mirror for me to use. Her friend gave me two huge lines which I sniffed through a rolled up dollar bill, one of the few I had. Somebody passed me a joint laced with PCP, and before I knew it I was plastered. The combination of the weed, heroin, PCP, Jack Daniels, and beer created an intoxicating effect like I had never experienced before. I felt like I was tripping on LSD without the side effects of nervousness.

The needle man with the long black beard asked, "So, who is this guy, Olivia, and what is he doing here?"

"I already introduced you," she answered. "What more do you want?"

"Well, he looks pretty young. I just want to know who I'm giving drugs to, that's all. You're not one of the patients from Menninger's, are you? Did she meet you at her job?"

"Ask her," I told him.

He stood up from his chair and looked me straight in the eyes. "No, I'm asking you. Tell me."

Olivia nodded her head at me behind his back, letting me

know it was alright to tell him the truth.

"She helped me escape today. I'm not a fucking looney, though."

"He's a cool guy," Olivia told him. "I really like him. He's got a great voice like Paul McCartney or John Lennon. They locked him up just because he kept running away from home and wouldn't go to school."

"I've got my diploma now, though," I said, "but they still won't let me go. I couldn't take it any more, so I just had to get away. I appreciate you people letting me hang out here with you for a while."

The guy sat back down at the table. "It's her house, man. Whatever she says, goes. If she says you're cool, then you're cool. Why don't you sit down and relax? I didn't mean to get on your case. I've been in trouble with the law, too. They busted me for dope a few times and threw me in Leavenworth. They held me there for six months, man. They they put me through the rehabilitation program which, as you can see, didn't work. I've never had problems with drugs, though, just with policemen."

Before long, Olivia took me upstairs to her bedroom. She grabbed my crotch and told me she wanted to feel my penis inside of her. This was it. We took off our clothes and climbed between the sheets. I performed cunnilingus on her for a half hour, really enjoying the taste and the sight of her wide open vagina. This was my first time and I wanted to make it last as long as possible. I had to stop several times during intercourse to prevent premature ejaculation. She waited patiently for me to calm down while I maintained her excited state by licking her clitoris and sliding one of my fingers in and out of her anus. She achieved orgasm swiftly after that with juices literally pouring forth to soak me and the sheets beneath us. I followed the example of the porno movies and pulled out at the moment of ejaculation, so she finished the job with her hands. I sprayed so hard that her breasts were completely covered with the precious fluid of life. Then I collapsed in her arms as we wallowed in a warm afterglow of mutual satisfaction. It was the best moment of my existence thus far, making everything else that was bad worth living through.

Despite the fact that we had made love, I still did not feel any real emotion for this girl. She was pretty, but I did not care much for her personality or the fact that she was a heroin addict. I did like her ideas about free love because that was the only kind I could afford back then. I probably would have stayed and fucked her a few more times if it weren't for a very bizarre event which occurred later in the evening when we went downstairs.

She had neglected to tell me that she was friends with one of the doctors on Hilltop at Menninger's. His first name was Kevin, and I honestly do not remember his last name, but all of the patients on the ward used to call him 'Turd' because he was always such an asshole. He looked like an old hippie and you would have thought he was a cool dude, but he enforced every rule vigilantly even when the other staff members might give us a break. He was particularly hardcore about the rules whenever he caught somebody with some dope.

I could not believe it when he came over to Olivia's house unexpectedly without even calling first. It was late at night. By then, I was passed out on the couch in the living room after watching TV for many hours. Olivia and a few other people continued shooting up in the kitchen. Kevin must have come in through the back door because he did not know I was there, and Olivia must have been too stoned to make the association between us. When I woke up, he had joined in on the party with everyone else. He finally saw me when he left through the front door, and he was so shocked that he did not say a single word to me. Instead, he just turned away and got out of there fast, knowing that he would be in big trouble if I ever told anyone at Menninger's about this.

The party was finally over. Everyone else left within a few minutes after that. I walked into the kitched and found Olivia sitting at the table with her head lying down amid all the paraphenelia. I shook her by the shoulders a few times to try to rouse her, but she was too far gone. I wanted to get out of there. She was obviously in no condition to drive a car, though, so I had to wait for her to get her act together. I drank another beer and watched the late news on television, figuring that I should be safe for a little while longer because if Kevin called the police he might be getting himself into a jam. At that moment, he was probably even more worried than I was. In any event, I wanted to be gone as soon as the sun came up.

Olivia drove me to Kansas City at six o'clock when she woke up. We had to stop for some coffee along the way or else she might have fallen asleep at the wheel. She apologized for what happened at her house and admitted she was having a hard time trying to think straight. When she dropped me off at the bus station, she gave me a hundred dollars and wished me good luck. I told her I would call her from Chicago when I arrived there just to let her know I was okay. I kissed her one last time before bidding her farewell.

Ten hours later I was back in the Windy City again. I made the rounds to visit my friends, which took a few days. They were glad to see me, but sorry to hear that I was on the run from the law again. Larry Maxwell took me out to dinner at Roselinni's in Northbrook where we saw the reliable pizza delivery man who sold marijuana. Then we went to the beach at Gilson Park in Wilmette where we proceeded to smoke our brains out. I slept at the house of Ben Parker on Private Road because he was a few years older and his parents did not mind if his friends stayed through all hours of the night, as long as we kept the noise down. Ben was a good buddy who frequently helped me out when I was on the streets. He prided himself on being an intellectual. We had long conversations about our philosophies, and he told me that he like me because I was a man of action instead of just a so-called intellectual who sat around talking all the time. He explained that many people of "expanded consciousness" wasted so much time rationalizing everything that they never really got anything done. I argued that all I was accomplishing was to get into more trouble. But he said I was proving something to Menninger's, my parents, and the law by being so rebellious. They would eventually realize that they were wasting their time with me and perhaps change their ways of dealing with problem children in the future. It was necessary for someone to stand up to fight against them so they would not become complacent and try harder to improve their system in the future. We were both sure that I had to be the most difficult patient Menninger's had ever dealt with.

In a desperate attempt to raise some quick money, I called Gordon Moore to see if there was any substance to his offer of getting me work as a male prostitute or actor in X-rated films in Las Vegas. He informed me that he was suffering from cancer, and he was no longer actively involved in the gay community. He offered me a job at his store in Winnetka, which I had to refuse for fear of being recognized by the police or a friend of my parents.

I met a Spanish woman of twenty-eight years who owned a framing shop in Hubbard Woods. She tried to hire me, too, but again I had to decline for the same reason. She asked me if I found her attractive, which I did. Then she invited me to her house in Buffalo Grove for drinks and an evening of sexual entertainment.

Her name was Brea Abello. She came here from Spain in 1971 as an immigrant with money she inherited from some wealthy relatives who passed away. To maintain a constant cash flow, she opened the Measure for Measure framery in 1975, which she sold in 1981 for $50,000, reaping a healthy profit because she did not even own the building where her business was located. But when she came to America she was overweight and found it difficult to get men interested in her. I was the first one to benefit from her good looks after she went on a strict diet. She was stunned to find out I was only sixteen and on the run. However, she liked me so much that I became her guest for the next week.

Brea put a sign on the front door of her store which read "On vacation one week." We spent that entire time locked up in her apartment exploring the realms of sexual fulfillment. Her expertise in this area was quite profound, and I felt like I was in heaven, making love as often as six times per day. She had a fetish for being tied down to her big brass bed while I did whatever I wanted with her for hours on end. Bondage appealed to my tastes, so I willingly gave her what she wanted. Meanwhile, I was developing my own fetish for ejaculating in her mouth and on her face, making her taste my warm semen every time I experienced orgasm. This made me feel superior and masculine, especially because she enjoyed bondage games. It seemed somewhat degrading for her, yet she agreed with me that we had never been so excited in all our lives. One day, because she said she wanted to feel my sperm inside of her for the purpose of variation, I stuffed her panties into her mouth and taped her mouth shut to stifle her loud moans of pleasure and pain. Then I forced my penis deep into her anus for a brutal exercise in sodomy.

As I still have so much more of this story to tell, I will concentrate further on the psychological reasons why some people get into sadomasochism later in the book. For now, let me move on to what led up to my arrest by the police in Evanston, Illinois.

A____ C____, who is now a fairly well-known actor, had stolen some marijuana from my friend Jake Ludlow's house. He was using this as a stake to start his own dealership. A____ and I were once classmates at Washburn School in Mr. Stanislaw's Advisory.

He knew me from there and sold me a small amount of weed even though he never liked me very much. I would not have bought it if I knew where it came from, which I did not discover until the next time I saw Jake Ludlow. Let me say here that when A____ became an adult, he never again participated in these kinds of activities. He was going through a rough transitional period in his life, and he managed to get it together pretty well later on, probably better than most of his old classmates. We were all proud of him when he landed a role in a movie called *M_____* by attending an audition at New Trier East, the Winnetka high school where many films have been made. He has since appeared in several other pictures, the best of which was *F_____*. Still, when we were kids he had no interest in the arts. All he wanted to do was participate in sports, and he would have been the last person you might have thought had a future in Hollywood.

Anyways, that night after getting the weed I went to the Evanston beach and smoked a few joints by myself. A helicopter flew overhead, shining a spotlight right onto my face. I knew it was the police. I suddenly panicked and ran north up the beach into the woods. When I reached Sheridan Road, two police cars pulled up. The officers jumped out and swiftly surrounded me. I could not get away. They threw me up against one of the vehicles, frisked me for weapons, and then slapped the familiar cuffs on my wrists. Soon I was paying another visit to the police station. It crossed my mind that nobody ever read me my rights or charged me with anything when I was arrested. I guess juveniles don't have any rights.

To dispose of the evidence, I had slipped out of the handcuffs and eaten my stash of marijuana while sitting in the back seat of the police car as they looked ahead through the windshield to the road. Alone in my jail cell later, I became so intoxicated that I slept for two days straight without even eating anything. When I woke up, the bars in the cells were moving and I saw hallucinations of patterns all over the wall. The guard wondered why I was laughing so hysterically since I was, after all, in jail. He did not think there was much to be amused about. The police ordered a drug test of my blood and urine. They found an incredible amount of THC in my bloodstream, plus traces of PCP and heroin. My probation officer was then called in to talk to me.

I was told that all of the beds at St. Joe's were filled, otherwise they would be sending me there. As expected, I was taken back to Kansas, but the lady probation officer warned me that if I was arrested again, in view of my long record, the judge might treat me as an adult and send me to jail. I yelled at her, demanding to be treated as an adult now so that I could be released from Menninger's. I promised to never get into any trouble again if they would just let me go. Of course, you can't bargain with a narrow-minded bureaucrat from Cook County. This insanity continued for another whole year before Menninger's finally gave up on me. I ran away two more times in the future, no longer threatened by the warnings of my probation officer, the police, and my parents. I simply had to go on challenging them, turning the Hilltop Unit upside-down in the process.

Chapter nine

I will skip ahead to July because the routine of solitary confinement was boring and predictable. Without Olivia there, I enjoyed no variation whatsoever. Olivia had been fired from the Hilltop Unit for undisclosed reasons. I felt that Kevin had told his superiors about me and her, yet I kept my mouth shut about seeing him at her house, and the subject never came up. I just sat in my room like a veg and waited for something to change. In July, Rachel came to visit me.

"So here you are again, living up to your nickname," she said. "Did you have a good time on your sojourn back to Chicago?"

"I'm not a virgin anymore," I informed her. "Does that make you want me any less?"

"Of course not, John. I hope it was a rewarding experience for you."

"Well, I'm sure you don't want to hear the details. How are things going with you? Do you like your new job?"

"It is nice working as a teacher with so many exceptional children. Most of the kids here are very intelligent. That's why they had a lot of trouble at school. Our standards of education are very low in this country. I think high school should be reduced to a two year term, and we should instill the desire to learn in children at a younger age."

I told her, "You can't force people to do anything. Those who want to learn will do it on their own, and the stupid kids will always be stupid. Nothing can change that. I've been through this subject a thousand times with you and everyone else here. Why don't you tell me what's going on in the outside world?"

"In the news the Iranians are calling for the death of the Shah. You know his son is here at Menninger's just to make sure nothing happens to him. Some terrorist would probably pay a lot of money for that information. Otherwise, Billy Carter is still acting like an idiot, punk rock is taking over as The Sex Pistols tour America, and David Bowie is scheduled to do a concert in Kansas City three weeks from now. I know how much you like Bowie, especially since you gave me his Ziggy Stardust album for my birthday. If I bought a pair of tickets for us to see the show, do you think you could control yourself long enough to get Dr. Petersen's approval?

"I could try, but I don't think he'd go along with it."

Petersen did go along with it, though, letting me outside for the first time in many weeks. He knew that he could trust me with Rachel. I'd never want to get her in any trouble, so there was no chance of me abusing her trust. Rachel had been honest with him about her feelings for me, though it never entered the official records. He was discreet about it, although he tried to use it to get me to open up to him, saying that if Rachel trusted him, then I should, too. With the Bowie concert in front of me like a carrot, I began going back to group meetings and personal therapy sessions with Petersen. He demonstrated that he was on my side many times, like when Carol Anne tried to get me into Biofeedback. He was sure it would have no value for me, nor did he think it would be healthy for me to have any outside influence over my emotions. Also, when the institution requested more X-rays to be taken of my head, he agreed with me that they were unnecessary and the subject was dropped.

Bowie's concert was not as crazy as I was hoping it would be. He no longer wore any of his bizarre androgynous costumes, discarding the image for a more mature, Frank Sinatra type of show. Still the music was as solid as ever, and he played for three hours with a brief intermission in the middle. Several Ziggy Stardust clones, including myself, inhabited the audience, but sadly our hero had already left us behind. We found it hard to believe how many old ladies came to see him. I was permanently converted to Alice Cooper after that. If Alice ever came out onstage in a three-piece suit and tried to act normal his audience would go berserk and kill him. But by selling out with commercial schlock, Bowie sold millions of records. His song "Fame" foreshadowed the disco days, and "Let's Dance" proved that he was only in it for the money. Some say that's all he was ever in it for, using rock music only as a tool for his own ego advertisement. He never listened to his critics though, or he would never have even done Ziggy in the first place. He must have felt satisfied that he had shaken the world once and did not see any reason to do it again. Besides, it's too much trouble.

After the show, Rachel took me out to dinner since I had paid for her to get the concert tickets. We talked about the music world, and I said that now with Bowie out of the glitter/punk movement there was an opening for a new outrageous star to take his place. What was there that had not yet been done onstage, especially with Alice Cooper as competition? I came up with the idea to change my name to Frankenstein, spreading the rumor to the media that I had been horribly disfigured in a terrible car accident and that my face was burned beyond recognition. I would wear a bondage mask onstage at all times, never revealing my true identity. During the show I would kill someone in the audience, who had to actually be a member of the road crew with fake guts stuffed into his stomach. I would cut him up with a huge knife and perform live cannibalism onstage to the accompaniment of the most bizarre music ever heard: Destructo-Rock.

Rachel was not quite amused by my sick sense of theatrical absurdity, and she found it hard to talk about seriously because she did not really believe that I would actually carry out such a thing. But "Destructo-Rock" was released on a record in 1980. It consisted of a three minute introduction followed by five minutes of distortion as my band and I smashed all of our instruments with the tape recorders rolling. The grotesque lyrics were written at this time during my stay at Menninger's.

I take my seat behind the wheel,
not sure exactly how I feel.
The tears are clearing from my eyes,
and now I don't give a damn who dies.
My fingers reach to turn the key.
I put on my shades so that I can see,
then press the gas down to the floor.
Everybody runs as I soar past them.
I've been up for three days now I think.
I know it's been a damn long time.
It's just impossible to sleep.
And now I'm coming down again.
So lower, darling, lower I sink,
with my drugs and grass and liquor and wine.
I simply cannot help but weep.
I think I'm losing my mind.
My life could end around this bend.
On the sidewalk I see a friend.
Behind me a policeman's lights.
I really don't want to hear my rights,
not that they'd read them to me anyway, you know?
Because my head is spinning around and round,
some bitch lay slain on the ground.

My eyes distort all that I can see.
I'm living death out on the street.

Although I personally think "Destructo-Rock" was the worst record I ever made, ironically it was the one that achieved cult status and has continued to sell through the years since its first pressing.

Now, back to where I left off. Rachel took me back to Menninger's later that night, and I tried to convince her to take me to her house so we could make love, forgetting about the fact that she was living with the secretary from Hillside, Elaine Nance. It was obvious that we could not go there when she reminded me. I suggested that we go to a motel, but she said that she could not do it yet, not until I was an "adult," released from the institution. I did not want her to end up like Olivia, so I left her alone and did not press it further. We only gave each other a warm kiss when she dropped me off outside the unit.

Back on Hilltop, the staff was showing me a little more consideration and letting me go out with a group on field trips to the movies. On a Sunday afternoon once we went on a cookout to a remote forest area about ten miles away. They let us go off hiking alone as long as we were back soon before they started getting worried about us. Nobody ran off. Instead, we were too preoccupied with a gigantic field of wild marijuana plants that we discovered in the wilderness. Some of them were ten feet tall! We smuggled about twenty-five pounds of the stuff back to the unit and had a mad smokefest for the next several weeks.

With the aroma of weed frequently stinking up the hallways, the Menninger's staff raided all our rooms and searched through everything. They found so much marijuana that it was hilarious, and some of us, like me, were clever enough to hide some of our stuff somewhere that they would never think of looking. I chose an air vent in the bathroom as my stash place, but kept enough in my room to make them think they had found all I had. Even after their search, we still had about ten pounds left.

Time passed more quickly and enjoyably when we were getting high all the time. We had to be more careful and smoke single hits out of homemade pipes, or some of us also created smokeless tokers out of empty tobacco canisters. I started playing music more seriously with Todd Darrel, as he calls himself now. We would smoke weed and write songs together, dreaming of the day when we would get out of there and make our bid for rock stardom. Lee (Okie from Oklahoma) started to play the drums in the music room, and he felt confident enough to back us up, so we started a band and practiced every day for a few weeks. Tara and a few other girls from Whitney came over to hear us play. We gave them a few good performances, although our skill was pretty primitive by professional standards. I realized that I had a lot of work to do if I really wanted to try to make a living in music. I always could have just been a vocalist or songwriter, but I really enjoyed wailing on the guitar, too. I concentrated to become a master of the instrument, gaining much of my knowledge from Jimmy Page of Led Zeppelin.

After being subjected to a few more surprise raids and searches, my supply of weed eventually began to dwindle. Also, I had been smoking my brains out constantly for weeks, not to mention the fact that I often ate large amounts when I wanted to get really fucked up. It so happened that I ran out of dope on the day when Rob Guillory was released. The day was awfully depressing because it is hard to say goodbye to someone you've been locked up with for such a long time. I was moved when he gave me a kiss on the lips as his farewell.

Rumours abounded through Menninger's that we were all a bunch of faggots living on Hilltop, what with me wearing makeup and the other patients imitating the way gay men talk just for fun. It was nothing but a joke that a lot of other people took seriously. No homosexual activity ever took place on Hilltop during the entire time I was there. In fact, most of us had centerfolds from magazines like Playboy and Penthouse hanging on our walls. We all wanted, desired, craved, and needed girls.

Even worse than being locked up on holidays was being there on my birthday. My privileges were revoked because I had been caught with dope so many times, and I had a fistfight with one of the social workers named Tom who was trying to stop me throwing raw eggs at him while the other patients laughed and cheered. I literally egged them on into a frenzy until the goons came to put a stop to it. Everybody was confined to their rooms for the night because the disturbance had approached riot proportions. I, however, was the fall guy who had to stay in solitary confinement again for displaying violent behavior. When the staff dragged me away to my room, I bit Roy Suvino on the arm, and I hurt a few other people with wild kicking and punching. It was the first time I had ever acted out violently against them with the actual intention of inflicting injury. Now they treated me like they thought I might be dangerous, and they were sure that with my deteriorating attitude I would try to run away again at the next available chance. They were right about that. But I didn't have to wait for a chance. I created my own exit.

Dan ('Crab') and I got the other patients to turn their music up real loud and make a lot of noise to cover out breakout. I took the metal bar out of my closet which was used to hang clothes on, and I used it with all my might to break through the supposedly bulletproof window in my room. Then I jumped out, falling about thirty feet to the ground below. My friend jumped out after me. Unfortunately, he did not land on his feet. His hands and arms broke the fall as he landed on top of the thick shards of broken glass. He cut himself up badly, yet he did not want to turn back, so he followed me through the cemetery into a wooded area where we hid for a few minutes and I used my socks to tie up his arms. This stopped the blood flow. When his cuts dried up, I removed the socks and put them back on my feet.

It was a strange coincidence that his name was also Dan, the same as the last person I had run away with. I cannot remember his last name, though, only that his nickname was 'Crab' because he always seemed to be in a bad mood and he hardly ever smiled. The two of us had previously sold our record album collections for a high price to a dealer in Topeka who specialized in obscure music by strange groups. Therefore we had a few hundred dollars between us. We bought two bus tickets to Chicago, and twelve hours later we were already there, partying with my friends.

Problems soon arose, however, as he was a diabetic who needed a shot of insulin every day or else he would die. He stole a few bottles of it from the refrigerator on Hilltop where it was kept, but he lost his wallet with the medical ID card, so we could not buy syringes at any drug stores. As a last resort, we went to Northwestern University Hospital to try to fix him up. I stayed in the waiting room while he went to talk to the doctors. He never came back. I waited there for over two hours with doctors and nurses and policemen all over the place. It became apparent to me that Crab must have been arrested when these people found out he was on the run from Menninger's. But I never should have left him alone because I found out later that he got lost and could not find his way back to where he was supposed to meet me. I guess his mind was clouded because he needed his shot. When he finally made it back to the waiting room I was gone, and he thought I had abandoned him. Crab proceeded to call Menninger's and turn himself in. Alone in a strange city, there was no place else for him to turn for help.

I was sure that Crab had received medical attention.

Otherwise, I would have been very worried about him. It was too bad he could not be with me to continue having a good time in Chicago. When I saw a midnight show of *The Song Remains the Same*, I really wished he was there because I had told him about the film many times. Also, I enjoyed many great afternoons with Jake, Felix, and David Ludlow at their house in Winnetka. Jake and I wrote a fantastic song called "One Fine Day with the Karma Man," another number which was later released on an album. Jake was and still is the fastest conga drum player in the world. He now owns his own company where he manufactures custom built percussion instruments with the highest quality wood. Concerning his background, his grandfather was once the host of the NBC Showcase TV program, and any Chicagoan should recognize his name because his family's company manages the S_____ and the J_____ Building, plus they own the Chicago S_____. The kids stood to inherit a fortune at the age of thirty, but the pressure from their parents to become respectable citizens was immense. Felix blew his brains out with a shotgun in 1981, leaving a suicide note designed to hurt everyone deeply. The family had been broken up by divorce, and the stepmother was the female equivalent of Edward, if you know what I mean. Again, disaster could have been avoided if the parents had not imposed their wills so strongly on the kids.

How could I visit the Chicago area without calling Brea Abello? She invited me back to her house in Buffalo Grove for another hardcore sex marathon lasting through an entire weekend. With her I became an experienced lover as she taught me everything she knew and reinforced my taste for the bizarre. I became convinced that there was nothing more beautiful in this world than a woman who would submit completely to her man, and vice-versa. For the first time, she tied me down to the bed and made me drink her urine as she pissed in my mouth. Initially, I was humiliated by it, but for reasons I did not understand it turned me on before it was over and I found myself with a raging erection which she climbed on top of, riding me until we exploded together with intense orgasmic pleasure. Strangely enough, images from my guided imagery session with Dr. Petersen kept flashing through my head while we were doing it. I did not realized the full significance of this at the time.

My latest runaway escapade ended when I went to the old stomping ground of Gilson Park in Wilmette on a sunny day with my friend Ben Parker. He still admired my rebellion, but I could tell he was starting to wonder how long it would go on, and how many more times I would be on the streets. We played Frisbee and drank a lot of beer until the sun began to set and he had to leave to pick up his girlfriend for a date. He had been seeing this girl for two years, but never gotten into her pants yet. He was sure this would be the night because his parents were out of town and he had the house to himself.

I stayed behind at the park to finish the case of beer, leaning up against a big tree. I fell asleep there for at least a few hours. It was dark outside when I came to my senses with the beam of a flashlight being directed right into my face. It was my friends, the police. They knew me by sight, now, for I had become a familiar fugitive to them. It was almost like a game to see how long I could go without being caught.

"Alright, Timmis. Get on your feet. You're under arrest... again."

The staff at Menninger's was starting to get noticeably uneasy with my presence there. Upon being returned to the Foundation, they put me in solitary confinement with nothing in the room except for a mattress on the floor. For the first week they would not even give me a book to read.

I was no longer asked to participate in the group meetings or in private psychiatric sessions with Dr. Petersen. At this point there was no treatment at all, just incarceration. The 'Veg' was back. It took a long time before I gained the trust of the staff once more. Thanksgiving and Christmas were upon us by then, and Rachel never visited me anymore. When I finally got my guitar back, and they were satisfied that I would not try to hang myself with the strings, I worked on perfecting the song I had composed with Jake Ludlow, "One Fine Day with the Karma Man." The lyrics are reprinted here for your reading enjoyment. As with my other songs, they offer additional insight into my way of thinking.

It was late in the afternoon when I awoke,
and reached to my nightstand for a smoke.
Realizing that it wasn't there anymore,
I decided to head down to the store.
I put on my boots and I combed my hair
then made my way on down the stairs.
A drunk was passed out in my doorway.
I just smiled sadly and then I turned away.
So as I was strolling on down the road
I met the Karma Man near his little abode.
"Come here and sit down beside me," he said,
as he withdrew a joint of Columbian red.
We enjoyed the herb to its fullest extent
and then retreated inside of his Boy Scout tent.
There was nothing in there but a small crystal ball
which sat on a table that had no legs at all.
I examined it closely finding no strings attached,
then I turned around and asked, "What is the catch?"
The Karma Man just smiled and took his seat on the floor,
and then he lit a cigar that had bought in the store.
He said, "Let us now deal with why you are here."
And I said, "Predict my future and I'll buy you a beer."

He fidgeted and fumbled and he quivered and quaked,
and I began to believe that he was a fake.
I said, "You're all washed up you silly old man,
and you're destined to die in the frying pan! Oh, yeah!"
I stepped back outside and much to my surprise,
everything had changed except the blue sky.
It was a barren desert stretching out for miles and miles.
There were weird wormy creatures there who wore plastic smiles.
In pure horror I dropped to my knees.
There were no cities, no forests or seas.
I looked up at the Karma Man silhouetted against the sun,
and I screamed in agony, "My God! What have you done?!"

Chapter Ten

1978 came, marking the beginning of another year at Menninger's. The entire holiday season was totally depressing, and I often found it hard to keep from crying because I felt like I was on the verge of a nervous breakdown. At Christmas everybody on the ward received numerous gifts in the mail from their relatives. All my mother sent me was a carton of cigarettes. She really cared about me, right? And my father didn't send anything. Rumor had it that Rachel was dating one of the other teachers at Southard School. Lee (Okie) was finally released when he turned eighteen and his juvenile record was filed away. I would miss him a lot because he was the one who showed me real hospitality and friendship when I first came to the Hilltop Unit. If I stayed there much longer I would soon become the senior patient. The only person who had been there longer than me now was Darrel Todd Johnson, or 'Egg' as we called him for reasons that I never really knew, for he had been given his nickname before I got there. It could have had something to do with his long red hair, or for the fact that if he did something stupid Lee would call him an egghead. But anyways, the holiday season really got me down, especially on New Year's Eve when I knew the whole rest of the world was having a party.

The longer they kept me there, the more hatred got built up inside of me until I actually contemplated the murders of my mother and stepfather. But I came to my senses, knowing that if I did this I would be ruining the rest of my life, and there were too many other things I wanted to do. I was always interested in many things. That is why I was able to keep my sanity during all those months in solitary confinement. Also, my interests kept me from getting into more trouble after I was released from Menninger's, although they never declared that I was cured, and they were sure I'd end up in jail. But I'm getting ahead of myself again.

I just wanted to point out that there would be a lot less trouble in this world if young people were interested in things. Nobody really believes that they can accomplish anything anymore, so they don't try. Our society has to be more open so kids can be whatever they want to be when they grow up, and they have to get help to accomplish their goals, real help that they can use instead of locking them up if they choose to be different. I am particularly disturbed today by the number of mental health and drug rehabilitation centers that have opened up, providing a 7-11 franchise-type of service with atmospheres so sterile that even laboratory mice would feel uncomfortable. The bottom line is that you cannot force your "help" on somebody who does not want it. In fact, if you commit one of your loved ones to an institution, you will make them resent you, even hate you, for the rest of their lives. I urge families to try every other avenue of pursuit before calling for outside assistance. That means love is the answer for us all. It always has been and it always will be. If you love someone you don't call for outside help and lay the problem on someone else. It's nobody else's business, anyways, so solve the problem yourselves! This, my friends, is basically the point of my whole book. I hope you understand it, although I don't think the people who make their livings from psychiatry and mental health care will be too pleased. They will argue in defense of their profession, but in your heart you know I'm right.

One of my favorite lines of all time is "Anyone who would

waste money on a psychiatrist ought to have his head examined."

When it comes to child psychology, the social workers are all too eager to go to work on somebody when they discover a classic case. Throughout the first eighteen years of my life they constantly tried to brainwash me into becoming what they thought a normal person was. My parents went along with everything because these people were professionals. All of their advice was acted upon in good faith. Perhaps Rachel was not far off base when she blamed everything on society. Looking at it this way would be easier for everyone because it relieves individual people of guilt and eliminates the need to get revenge. But we all have to work to make society better. If we continue on our present course, we will create a whole generation of people with no hope, and no ambition but to destroy everyone around them.

One of my last group meetings was in January of 1978 with my mother, Edward, and my sister Valerie who came to visit me when she was released from the institution in Pennsylvania. I pointed out that if she was having problems, too, then I could not be entirely at fault for all the trouble in our family. If Valerie was experiencing the same psychological disorders as I was, then we were obviously reacting against the negative environment around us. My sister, looking for an excuse to blame her drug habit on, had claimed that my father and Edward had both molested her at different times. I am sure she was lying to grab the spotlight away from me and direct it onto herself. She has consistently used this story for nearly two decades to obtain sympathy from doctors who lock her up in hospitals. She has been taken care of by outside forces through most of her adult life. Valerie was committed again within a few months of her visit to Menninger's.

In this group meeting my "family" was bickering back and forth amongst themselves while I sat there like a vegetable, living up to my nickname. The doctors finally got their first look at the kind of madness that was really going on in my home before I had been locked up. My mother tried to convince them that while we may have been abused children, neither my father or Edward ever molested us. The most they ever did was hit us or kick us around the room when we were being bad and deserved it. My mom said that once my father picked me up by the feet when I was an infant, holding me upside down over an open toilet bowl. He dunked my head inside it, flushing the toilet at the same time so that the water was swirling around me. He yelled, "If you don't behave I'm gonna flush you down!" As soon as my mother told us this, I remembered it, a long-lost memory that haunted my subconscious.

"Damn you!" I shouted. "God damn you to hell! Why did you have to tell me about this? What bearing could it possibly have on my life now except to make me feel bad and hate my father? You fucking pigs! I'm sick of this shit! You all wallow in the excrement of your own existence as you spew forth on the foul-smelling vomit of hypocrisy!"

The meeting broke up on that note as I stormed out of the Caulder Building and walked back to Hilltop by myself with Dr. Petersen trying to catch up with me. Being an older gentleman, he did not want to run, and with my long legs I can walk very fast, so he did not get a chance to talk to me until I sat down on the front steps of the Hilltop unit and waited for him. He approached, out of breath, then sat down next to me on the steps.

"I thought you were going to run away again," he said.

"I might. You know you can't hold me no matter how hard you try."

"I know you don't like what your mother said in the meeting, John, and it must be very humiliating for you. But her story is valid if you compare it to the images you experienced in your first session with me. Remember when I tried to hypnotize you and it didn't work, so we did the guided imagery instead?"

"Yeah. Yeah. I remember."

"And you said you used to have similar recurring nightmares about the same things, right? It seems to me that your biggest fear in life, the one at the root of everything, is your fear of being flushed down the toilet. That was a traumatic experience for you as a child, and you blocked it out of your mind all these years. It has become a metaphor in your subconscious mind, symbolizing your more realistic fear of being consumed by everything around you. John, you don't want your life to go down the drain. I think if you would continue to work with us, then we would be able to help you."

"Sure, Dr. Petersen, but what is the use of going through this stuff again and again and again? You already have your answers. Write them down in your log book and consider my dase closed. Why don't you sign my release papers and let me out of here?"

He replied, "Because if I did that I would have to state that you are cured, and I can't do that because if you are released and then self-destruct or cause harm to other people, then we could be sued for damages."

"Great, so I'm stuck here until September 21st, 1979 when I turn eighteen. By then I might really be a fucking psychopath. Thanks a lot."

"It's not so bad, John. It may seem like an eternity now, but ten years from now you'll look back at this and laugh at yourself for thinking that this was so terrible."

"No, I won't," I assured him. "Believe me, I won't."

"The decision to hold you here is for your own good. All decisions concerning your life are."

"You make decisions about my life? Think about that. *My* life! Nobody should be able to make any decisions about my life except me!"

"Look, John, many times I've talked with your parents

about your future. They have great plans for you. When you turn eighteen, Edward would like you to go back home and maybe work at his publishing company. He would even like to give you the money to go to college. Lots of kids would give their right arm for a chance like that."

"Find one, then."

"What did you say?"

"You said lots of kids would give their right arm for the chance, so I told you to find one. I don't want it. I have my own plans for my future, and they don't include going back to school."

"Well, I've never heard of such ingratitude..."

"Bullshit. You should know me better than that by now, Doc."

"Well, then what do you want to do when you get out of here, John?"

"I wanna be a rock and roll star. Do you think that's too far-fetched?"

"No. James Taylor was here once, and so were two members of the rock group Kansas. They were once troubled young men like yourself who dreamed of stardom, and they made their dreams come true, so maybe you can, too."

I was surprised by his encouragement of my goal, and any anger I felt towards him subsided at that time. Like everyone else, he was just doing his job, although he did it better than most. We went back to the unit and continued with our daily routine. That night, he stayed and had dinner with the patients in the cafeteria, generally creating an atmosphere of optimism among the group. He was a pretty far-out old man who could relate to the guys on Hilltop and gain their friendship.

In February, they started letting me go out on field trips with the group again. I suppose they were asking for trouble, but it was also created without any help from me.

One of the staff members, whose name I cannot reveal because

I made him a promise, took three patients, including myself, to his house one night for an evening of partying. He was a black man about thirty years old who had been a troubled youth himself, and he knew we would appreciate gettin away for a short time to drink some beer and smoke some weed. We also thought it was nice that he treated us like adults and trusted us to keep a secret. As a result, he was the only social worker on the unit that we really respected, and we never gave him a hard time like we did with everybody else. On another occasion, we sniffed PCP and went to see a screening of *Close Encounters of the Third Kind*. He probably would have continued to party with us if it weren't for the fact that I got sick and had to go to the bathroom to throw up several times. One of the other patients flipped out later in the evening and smashed everything in his room becacuse he wanted to go home. The PCP must have triggered this violent outburst because he was usually a very mild-mannered kid. But PCP, or "angel dust" as it is known on the street, will do that to you, and it is certainly one of the most dangerous drugs on the market.

It was around this time that a new social worker named Dr. Cahn started working on Hilltop. He was a big, fat man who could probably roll faster than I can run. The man graduated from college in Wichita, Kansas, where his professor had been Duane, Jones, the Negro star of *Night of the Living Dead*. Cahn seemed like a faggot to me and everyone else, but he had a jolly personality which made all the patients enjoy being with him. He started hanging around me much of the time, to the point where I didn't have any privacy when he was on duty. A few times he walked into my room without knocking first and caught sight of me in the nude, which is probably what he wanted.

I voiced my dissatisfaction with him to Carol Anne and Brian, two other social workers on the unit. They told me to be patient with him since he was new to Menninger's, and they were certain he was not a homosexual. When I saw him after that, I tried to be more friendly with him. He started taking me outside for long walks on the Menninger grounds. We talked about many things, but the subject of homosexuality always came up because he had an extraordinary interest in discussing it. He became aware of some of my previous experiences by reading the Hilltop log books. Also, there were a few times when I spoke candidly in group meetings after I was sure the other patients respected me enough not to condemn me for it. Not only that, I was still wearing makeup sometimes, trying to look like Mick Jagger, the singer of The Rolling Stones, in the movie *Performançe*. All this combined to make him very interested in my case, only because he himself was a homosexual.

There was a girl on one of the other units in my building who started calling me on the telephone to talk to me. Her name was Lorna Lynn, and she was a tall blonde bombshell who could make any man become a slave to desire. She had previously been the girlfriend of Todd Darrel, but when he started getting too serious about her she backed off. Yet she was convinced that I was the boyfriend she had been looking for, and she wanted to go all the way with me if we could get out of the institution. We saw each other during meals in the cafeteria, too, and we planned to run away together when she was on a weekend pass to visit her family in Topeka. She said that she could get about five hundred dollars, which would be enough for us to go to Chicago and get an apartment. I had to escape from Menninger's and meet her at a designated time by the baseball diamond across the highway.

It was Dr. Cahn whom I chose to be my victim, but not without provocation. On a stroll through the Menninger grounds one afternoon, he pressed the homosexuality subject harder than ever before, like he was leading up to something. I explained that, at best, I might have some bisexual tendencies, though my main interest was in women. I said that femininity was one of the few beautiful things left in this world, and I was merely imitating it with my image that I would later use onstage at concerts in much more extreme form. At this point in my life, however, I was trying to be more subtle about it because I don't believe makeup does its job right if other people can tell you are wearing it. They should just naturally think that you are good-looking. I thought men had the potential to be just as beautiful and interesting to look at as women are.

Cahn must not have believed what I told him, that I was not really homosexual, or else he simply did not want to believe it since he found himself attracted to me. Whatever the case, he offered me twenty dollars to perform oral sex on him which he proposed that we could do in the empty recreation room on Hillside. I was not at all surprised by his advance, for I had been expecting it, even counting on it. For the first time in my life, I beat someone up. I punched him in the stomach and kicked him to the ground, calling him a pig and telling him that I was running away with Lorna Lynn. If that didn't make him think twice about my being homosexual, then what would? He struggled to his feet and vowed not to let me get away, but I hit him again and again until he finally released his hold on me. He got down on his knees, keeling over onto the pavement in pain. I ran off through the cemetery for the last time.

Lorna met me at the baseball field as scheduled. She brought a six-pack of beer and a few joints of grass for us to smoke in celebration of the escape. I told her about Cahn, and she found it difficult to believe. The two of us sat in the grass for about an hour getting high, feeling the breeze, and kissing each other. Luckily, I remember it was an extremely warm day for that time of year, like God was on our side, blessing us with nice weather.

One of Lorna's friends from town gave us a ride to Lawrence,

Kansas where we felt a little more safe. In Topeka, the law was searching every street for us, and Cahn probably told the Menninger staff that Lorna and I were together, though he should have just kept his mouth shut. For some reason, I never told anyone about his sexual advances toward me. In retrospect, it does seem outrageous. At the time, though, it seemed almost normal, like just another of so many offbeat incidents which comprised my life. I am not sure how long he continued to work at Menninger's after I was gone. He should never have worked there at all.

Lawrence is a college town with a lot of bars, sporting events, and a theater called the Lawrence Opera House where we saw Jeff Beck and the Jan Hammer Group in concert. After that, we took a Greyhound bus to Kansas City. This was the transfer point for our bus to Chicago. On the second bus, we sat in the back seats and kissed each other for hours during the long trip. The two of us went into the lavatory to smoke the last of our marijuana, too. It was a relaxing journey that we really enjoyed.

When we arrived in Chicago, she was impressed by the gigantic scale of the downtown area. The recently completed Sears Tower was the tallest building in the world. I'm sure she felt somewhat dwarfed by it, and I could tell that she didn't like it very much since she was a country girl. Still, we went up to the north side and rented a small kitchenette apartment on Winthrop Avenue. It was in a fairly dangerous part of the city with plenty of gang activity in the streets. We did not feel comfortable going out at night, but we went on long walks despite this fact because we were both sick of being cooped up inside. Luckily, nothing bad ever happened. On our first night there, we went out to get a bottle of wine, and we got drunk at the Farwell beach. When the temperature outside went down too low, we went back to the apartment with the intention of making love. She thought I was still a virgin because I did not pounce on her immediately. I must admit that I was a bit nervous with her. She was the first girl my age that I had ever been with in this situation. I had an LSD flashback that produced a hallucination of her with a witch's face, and it turned me off completely. I did not tell her about it, but she knew something was wrong. We spent the rest of the evening merely holding each other tightly in bed until we fell asleep. In the morning, I found that she had taken off all of her clothes. I licked her swolled clitoris so that she could have an orgasm, yet I still did not have intercourse with her.

I went out to find a job early that morning. There were openings at Manpower, a temporary help agency. They put me to work in a latex factory which specialized in the manufacture of dildos (artificial penises) and an assortment of shoe pads. There I met a man who was actively involved in Chicago's gay community. He convinced me that I was much too good-looking to be working in a factory. After we were done with the job, he took me to a bar at the intersection of Clark and Diversey where young men were making fortunes selling their love by the hour. For the third time, I was offered a part in a homosexual X-rated movie. The job paid two hundred dollars for one hour's work. This time I accepted the offer, and I went back to the apartment to change into some nicer clothes. Then I was supposed to meet the producers at a video store on the south side of the city.

When I told Lorna the truth about what I was doing, she said "We don't need money that bad, John. I still have more than two hundred dollars left. That should be enough to last us until you get your first paycheck."

I replied, "I don't want to work in a factory for a lousy five dollars an hour. This is a good opportunity for us to get ahead. Besides, these people think I could be a big star in X-rated films, and not just in gay films. Nothing you can say is going to stop me. I have to leave to meet them right now. You wait here and I promise I'll be back in a few hours."

The video store on the south side was located in an otherwise abandoned building in a horrible neighborhood that looked like it had barely survived a devastating nuclear blast. Garbage was everywhere, and big rats could be seen in the alleyways. There was not a single white person on the streets except for myself. I was scared, even a little repulsed, but I went ahead and made the film against my better judgement. The three other actors were all black men, too. The only white in the crowd was one of the cameramen. We all went upstairs to a loft area which was completely empty save for a mattress, some lights, and two Super 8 movie cameras set up at opposite angles. The film we made is probably a collector's item now, especially amongst those familiar with my later work in legitimate movies and the music business. Fortunately, I have never seen any copies of it for sale. The company that made it went out of business in 1980 after being busted by the FBI for bootlegging copyrighted motion pictures from Hollywood on videotape. Looking back, I think this was the dumbest thing I have ever done. Those bastards could have killed me and nobody would have been able to solve the crime.

That night, after collecting my money, I was apprehensive about seeing Lorna back at the apartment. I procrastinated by going to a restaurant for dinner, and I called my mother from a payphone to let her know I was alright. She knew Lorna was with me, warning that this girl was dangerously unstable. She suggested that I talk Lorna into returning to Menninger's for further treatment.

"What about me?" I asked.

"It's over, John," my mother told me. "Menninger's has given up on you. They don't want you back. Thank God your period of probation is up, too, or else they'd probably be sending you to jail."

"So, I'm free?"

"Yes, John. None of us believe that it would be beneficial to find another institution to take care of you."

"I don't need for anyone to take care of me, Mom. I'm not a little child anymore, even though I'm not recognized as an adult by the law."

She said, "I know that, John. We still want to help you, though. Why don't you come up to the house tomorrow so we can talk about what you want to do in the future?"

"Alright, but what about Lorna?»

"You are harboring a fugitive right now. They want you to take her back to Menninger's when you go to get all the stuff you have in your room there. You could jeopardize your own freedom if you don't do this. I'll pay for your airline tickets if you make the right decision. When you come to the house tomorrow, bring Lorna with you. Otherwise, don't bother coming at all. Do you understand me?"

"Yeah. I can have my freedom if I give up my girlfriend, right?"

Of course, I went along with what they wanted. The prospect of diving right into more trouble after just getting Menninger's off my back did not appeal to me. I had to do a lot of talking with Lorna to convince her that this was the best thing for both of us. I promised to keep in close touch with her. If she wanted to live with me after her release, then I would go along with that, too. She hesitantly went with me on the train up to my parents' house in Winnetka where we ate well and drank a lot of wine. For the first time in my life, my mother and Edward treated me with respect. It was a startling change which I really appreciated. They did not even object when Lorna and I wanted to sleep in the same room.

Another day later, we returned to Topeka via the airport with my mother and Edward. Spring was moving in and the weather was getting nicer all the time. Kansas was experiencing very hot temperatures. The air conditioner in our cheap rented car did not work, either. I began to sweat heavily as we entered the Menninger grounds. I was afraid my parents might pull a fast one and leave me there, but this did not happen. Lorna held my hand firmly, and I gave her one of the silver bracelets I wore on my wrists as a gift to remember me by. She put it on, then smiled genuinely with affection. Her lips met mine for the last time in the back seat as we approached the building and the doctors came out to greet us. It was an extremely difficult moment for me, and Lorna made matters worse by bursting into tears as the staff took her away. It all seemed so sad, yet I was positive that these hard times were coming to a close for me.

The patients on Hilltop were all very surprised to learn that I had been released. I told them this proved if they fought back hard enough, then the doctors at Menninger's would eventually give up when they realized they had been beaten. I still had a little more than a year to go before my eighteenth birthday, time which I would have spent locked up if I did not resist it. I felt like I had achieved a victory when I walked out of there that afternoon. To show that I had not changed a bit, and that I was still as wild as ever, I played my song "In the Can/The Mental Institution Blues" for everyone, ending the number by smashing my guitar into little pieces. Then I said goodbye and went outside, never to return. They had to clean up the ruins of my battered guitar themselves. This was the crucial day I had been waiting so long for. I could not let it pass without creating some sort of disturbance to distinguish it. I felt great, and I was looking forward to carrying on with the rest of my life.

Epilogue

Things did not go as smoothly as I had hoped after my release. I went to visit the grandmother on my father's side of the family in Warren, Pennsylvania. My other three grandparents were all dead. Grandma Doll used to joke with me when I was a kid, telling me that I was her favorite grandson even through she did not have any others to choose from. Now, I joked with her that she was my favorite grandmother, and she knew she was the only one left. I had a nice time with her, but my sister Valerie was living with her at the time, causing problems left and right. I was dumb enough to let her rope me into bringing her back to Chicago for an ill-fated visit with my mother and stepfather.

Valerie proceeded to destroy my home and all of my plans by getting into a fight with me on the night when my friends were throwing a welcome home party for me at the house. She demanded that I let her use my electric guitar, although I was already playing it to entertain my friends. For no good reason, she slapped me across the face as hard as she could. I got mad and punched her in the stomach so hard that she was nailed to the wall behind her. Edward saw this, so he rushed to break it up by grabbing a hold of me and twisting my arm, automatically assuming the whole thing was my fault. I was not a little punk who could be pushed around by him anymore, though. I wrestled with him until I had him down on the floor in the kitchen. Then I grabbed a whiskey bottle by the neck, broke it on the counter, and pointed the broken glass directly at his face. I told him that if he ever touched me again I would kill him. I walked out of the house and took all my friends with me, knowing that I was out on the streets again.

I never forgave my sister for the incident. When I talked to her on the phone a year later, all she had to say about it was, "Too bad we weren't on TV. It would have made for a great episode on a soap opera."

Today, Valerie rots in a state mental institution where she continues to play games with everyone around her. On other occasions, she has been known to attack me with a pair of scissors, or once she tried to push our stepmother down the stairs at the house in Athens. She drove her husband George away by acting like a maniac all the time, and most recently she even cut up her boyfriend with a razor blade. Obviously, my sister cannot cope with the turmoil inside her head, and she needs to be institutionalized. Valerie demonstrates that there are cases where clinical treatment is the only way to go. After all, they can't give her the death penalty just for being crazy. If she ever reads this book she will probably be disturbed by it, not that she isn't already disturbed, anyways.

For the next three months, I lived under a bridge in Winnetka like a troll and worked in a gas station up to twelve hours a day, saving money to get an apartment. Sometimes I slept at the beach for a change of scenery. Around this time, my parents' house was burglarized, and the thief tried to steal my electric guitar. My stepfather came home while this person was still in the house, so the thief had to escape by jumping off the second floor balcony, breaking his leg in the process. I know he broke his leg because I know who did it: a kid from my old school days named Christian Baker, whom I mistakenly told that my parents frequently left town on business. The house was dark, and he was no real friend of mine, so he attempted to rob the place when he thought it was empty. Years later he apologized to me and said he was going through a rough period in his life, living on the streets as I was. But my mother and Edward repeated the same mistake they had made before by accusing me of the burglarly, and they threw away all my possessions out in the backyard where they were ruined by the rain.

I tried renting a house in Topeka with Lorna after she was released. This never worked out, though, because we found out that our interests were too different. For one thing, she loved disco music, which was like the kiss of death as far as I was concerned. When Rachel Couenneoeur heard that I was living in town with Lorna , she became almost unreachable and refused to go out on a date with me.

After my seventeenth birthday, I went back to Chicago again and got an apartment in Rogers Park, sharing it with a friend from Wilmette named Paul Graham. He was a college intellectual who studied engineering. He invented the "Hermaphrodite Wrench" which I named for him as it had the capability to accommodate both male and female fixtures. Paul also followed obscure music religiously. We had many great, lengthy conversations about the future of rock and roll, and what we considered to be important about it. At this time, I had my first publicity photographs taken at a professional studio, and I was busy writing new songs for a demo tape to send to the record companies. Paul was always interested in poetry. He had many useful suggestions concerning the rhythm and pacing of syllables. My best record of all was written and recorded when I lived in Rogers Park with him. It was called *The Monitors*, and it featured the most hard-hitting lyrics I had yet composed, dealing directly with my bad opinion of society.

I've had enough of being pushed around against my will.
You must be completely shattered, eating all those pills.
But maybe we can break away instead of standing still.
THE MONITORS: "WE ARE THE ONES IN CONTROL,
AND THERE'S NOTHING YOU CAN DO.

YOU MUST SIMPLY PLAY THE ROLE
IN LIFE THE WAY WE TELL YOU.
IF YOU REFUSE TO CONFORM,
THEN WE WILL SIMPLY SEND YOU AWAY.
RISE ABOVE THE SOCIAL NORM
AND ALL YOUR LIFE YOU'LL PAY."
How many pawns have you employed?
With how many people have you toyed?
And how many minds have you destroyed?
Now you've taken all I've got
and left me here to rot.
I'm your heel without a meal.
I'm hungry, but I don't want to steal.
What's your prize in the end,
when you've abused every friend,
run out of rope and beyond hope,
and the world's strung out on dope?
How many minds have you destroyed?
With how many people have you toyed? ·
How many pawns have you employed?
THE MONITORS: "WE ARE THE ONES IN CONTROL,
AND THERE'S NOTHING YOU CAN DO.
YOU MUST SIMPLY PLAY THE ROLE
IN LIFE THE WAY WE TELL YOU."
But you are easily expendable!
I wouldn't miss you a bit!
Don't try to act respectable!
Your sports coat doesn't even fit!
You fools! Watch me burn! Ha! Ha! Ha! Ha! Ha! Ha! Ha!

The Monitors was recorded at QR Studios in Evanston, Illinois
and released to a lukewarm reception in the beginning of 1979.

Record sales were slow, but I did enjoy some radio airplay and a few good notices in local newspapers which declared it to be the best debut by a Chicago artist. The flip side of the disc was an odd number called "Disciples of Rock and Roll," about my concept of starting a rock and roll church where people could worship their idols like other people worship God. The idea was stolen by another Chicago band called Ministry. They went on to get a lucrative recording deal with a major label.

My second record, *Waiting for the CTA*, was lifted by Chicago disc-jockey Steve Dahl because his manager was at the studio when I recorded it. This was a novelty song about waiting for a bus or train in the Windy City, and it would mean nothing to anyone outside Chicago. But the CTA was on strike when the record came out, so I anticipated decent sales. Dahl's manager offered to purchase the rights from me. I refused, though, so they changed the words around a little and made their own record which, by the way, sold thousands of copies on the strength of Dahl's ability to promote it through his radio station, WLUP. I probably could have sued him and won the case, only I didn't have enough money to hire a lawyer.

In 1979, I put a band together to perform my material live. We called ourselves The Clones at first, then Clone, then Frankenstein, then J.T. 4, then J.T. 4 and Cosmic Lightning, changing our name so often because no club would hire us more than once. We had a bad habit of smashing all our instruments and starting riots. No big money or recording contract ever came our way, although we did achieve a notorious reputation and cult status. The bad eventually broke up as I was no longer able to afford paying the musicians.

It was towards the end of this difficult year when I started having an affair with an older married woman named Stacy Kircher. She was as pretty as a model or movie star, yet she had no aspirations to become famous. In fact, her only talent lay between the sheets in bed. Being a horny young stud, I humped and pumped that lady constantly through the entire length of our relationship. She divorced her husband and moved into a new apartment with me before Christmas. Her daughter, Marsha, was eleven years old, and so I became a stepfather, believe it or not! We raised the kid through her rough teenage years and had virtually no problem with her because we did not make the same mistakes you have seen carried out earlier in this book. I did not pretend to be her father, nor did I act like a traditional authority figure. Our rules were very loose, as you might imagine. Without anything to rebel against, the child grew up to be a fine young lady with no psychological problems.

Having found it hard to make a living in music in Chicago, which is a business town (they pick paper up in one place and move it to another place), I started working for the Chicago Fraternal Order of Police. The job allowed me to work as much as twelve hours a day as a fundraiser for the union. With all that overtime, they paid me a handsome check every week, and I saved my money to make more records like *Destructo-Rock* under the name Frankenstein. Without a full-time band or proper management, however, my dreams of stardom began to fade away.

I turned to writing as a way of releasing my creative energy. Six novels were pounded away on my typewriter, all of them rejected by the publishing companies and agents I sent them to. The closest I ever came was with a nonfiction reference book called *The Complete Dictionary of Horror and Science Fiction in the Movies*. The publishing house that was seriously considering it changed their minds negatively when they had the simultaneous opportunity to print Leonard Maltin's compilation of reviews which covered every movie currently on TV. I tried writing a screenplay for Vincent Price, which he accepted after turning down every script submitted to him for the last decade. Yet I was never able to find a producer who would back the project.

Beaten again, I stubbornly turned to film-making. My first feature-length picture was called *Nightmare City*, a George Romero ripoff about the country being taken over by killers who had orders from the government to exterminate all undesirable citizens of America. A small number of videotapes was released independently by my own Destruction Productions. This was in 1982. I adapted some of the ideas for a 1985 horror quickie called *Cannibal Orgy*, which also had a limited release on video. That same year, I put together an eight-piece band made up of professional studio musicians, and we made a concert movie called *Cosmic Lightning*. The film cost $11,000 to produce. All of the finances were supplied by me. I was sure that such a monumental achievement would attract the attention of the record companies. After serious consideration, the presidents of several major labels passed on the material. The sound quality wasn't good enough, they said, failing to take into account the fact that it was recorded live. I spent another two thousand rerecording the same songs in the studio, but they turned me down again, by now probably getting a little annoyed by my constant pestering.

`In 1986, I produced a documentary called *The History of Rock and Roll* which has sold mildly on videotape and been screened on nonprofit cable TV channels. I also worked as a paid director for L.D. Groban, a local artist, who wanted me to make the longest movie in the world, basing it on his 4,000 page poem, "The Cure for Insomnia." We were published in the Guinness Book of World Records for this feat, achieving motion picture history. *The Cure for Insomnia* was premiered at the School of the Art Institute of Chicago. The picture is eighty-five hours long, consisting of L.D. Groban reading pages of his poem, interspersed with scenes of my band in concert, plus bizarre video imagery and some X-rated footage. It is funny how my worst creative projects are the ones most appreciated by the public. People look for hidden meaning in the film, thinking I'm a disturbed genius or something, but there are no hidden meanings at all. It's just abstract art, like the paintings of Salvador Dali. Whatever you see in it or get out of it is entirely up to you. All I did was provide the images.

Still, I found it hard to get work in the business, and I was always the first one to get rejected when I went to film auditions as an actor. They took one look at me and said, "Out!" Only someone who is really dedicated to his craft could continue against such opposition. But I was used to having the odds against me, so I never gave up hope. I stopped throwing money out the window trying to promote myself, though, and concentrated on having a better life at home. At least I could achieve sexual satisfaction. Stacy was my consolation prize.

My taste for the bizarre increased, especially when Marsha moved out at the age of eighteen and was married to a Mexican illegal immigrant who was able to buy a gun permit before he even had his citizenship papers. His name was Jesus, and he was a hard worker, content just to obtain the material things in life and have children. Soon my wife was a grandmother! Can you imagine me, with everything you know about me, having grandchildren coming over to my house and being asked to babysit? When one of the kids accidentally erased a master videotape of mine, I vowed never to let them into my house again. Even though Stacy was working at the Board of Trade, I paid the rent, so I made the decision and she had to live by it, otherwise I would leave her flat.

With new privacy after the departure of her daughter, Stacy and I experimented with the dark side of sex. We no longer had to go out to motels, so our encounters were much more frequent. bondage games became a regular part of our lives. I made a deal with her that I would take her to Paris if she would let me make a pornographic movie with her. My next choice as a profession was as the director of X-rated films.

What is most discouraging to me about the X-rated movie business are the prevailing social misconceptions concerning bondage, gang-bangs, rape fantasies, etc. It has never been, nor will it ever be, my purpose to depict women as mere subordinates to men. The pictures and films that I produced and directed, even participated in, are not about that. I designed them for men and women to whom bondage games and S&M are important mutual diversions. I tried to appeal to the male or female adult whose basic nature identifies with the female in bondage and craves to experience those offbeat sensations either for deeply psychological reasons, or just because it actually feels good. Therefore, bondage is essentially a gentle act used by lovers to enhance their emotional and physical closeness. It has more to do with being wanted then being abused. She gets to belong utterly and completely to the man she loves, and to be adored for what he perceives as the prettiness of femininity and her dependance on him. With this philosophy, you can see that bondage has nothing to do with demeaning anyone. It must be totally and absolutely a bilateral activity, otherwise it becomes an act of degradation and humiliation which I would not want to have anything to do with.

All this stated, let me jump ahead to 1988 and say that my wife did leave me after nearly a decade of marriage when I went ahead and released our first X-rated film, *The Love Quest*. Having enjoyed the first commercial success of my career, I was eager to make another movie soon, and she decided that she did not want to become a porno actress. If I forced her into it, then I would be doing what I just said I was against, so we called it quits and went our separate ways. We had a bad fight when she tried to find and destroy the master negative of the movie, but I kept it in a safety deposit box at my bank along with her signed contract.

In 1989, on my way to promote some new records in Las Vegas, I paid a visit to the Menninger Foundation for the first time in eleven years. Only a few people from my past still worked there, like Roy Suvino, Carol Anne, Elaine Nance, Dr. Petersen, and a few of the receptionists. I gave them copies of my records and requested that some of them be taken to the patients who were now on Hilltop. Maybe they would be inspired by them to try to pursue their own dreams and not give up in the face of opposition. If one of the patients could be so inspired, then that was a spiritual reward worth more than money.

Elaine Nance had been promoted and was now working in the Caulder Building as an administrator or something like that. She had her own office and looked very comfortable when I stopped by for my surprise visit. She remembered me right away by the eyes, or so she said.

"I can't believe that you remembered me after all these years," she told me, and put her arms around me. "It's been a long time."

"How could I forget you, Elaine ? After all, you were Rachel's roommate, right? She talked with me about you a few times, and I'm sure she told you about me, and how we felt towards each other."

"Yes. She told me. She was always upset that things never worked out between you, but you were in an impossible situation, and then you got married. She was sure that she'd never hear from you again. Now, she's living in Alaska where she built her own cabin and teaches school."

I smiled, remembering that this was always Rachel's dream. "That's a pretty bold thing to do, going there all by herself. She always had a strong will, though, and I could tell she was extremely independent."

Elaine said, "She never felt a need for anyone except you."

"Do you know an address where I can reach her?"

"No, but Dr. Petersen or somebody else might. Why don't you leave your address and phone number with me and I'll try to get it to her, okay? Maybe you two can get together for a reunion someday."

"I hope so," I replied. "That would tie up a bad loose end in my life which has been like a thorn in my side for years. The only woman I ever really loved was Rachel. You wanna know what true love is? It's wanting someone year after year, not being able to have them, but still wanting them desperately until that person becomes almost like a superhuman figure. That's the way I still feel about Rachel. I was recently divorced because I found that I really did not love my wife. I was just using her as a sex object for the last decade!"

"You were married that long? It seems hard to believe. You still look so long, and you have the bluest eyes in the world."

"You're too kind, Elaine . Thank you very much. That means a lot to me. Do you know how long it's been since someone said that to me? Well, it's been a long, long time."

"Does it seem strange to be back here after so many years, John?"

"Yeah, it sure does. Not much has changed, really, except they built a housing development next to the cemetery. The people who live there must feel a bit weird with a cemetery on one side of them and the psycho wards on the other side of them. I don't think I'd want to live there, but they look like nice apartments."

She asked me, "How do you feel about the past now? Do you have any good memories about Menninger's, or are they just all... bad?"

"Mostly bad, except for Rachel. She kept me from going crazy most of the time. Towards the end, though, we inevitably drifted apart as I knew we would when she left Hilltop and started working at Southard School."

"Don't you feel bitter about it now, any of it?"

"Bitter? No. Why should I feel bitter? They took a long time out of my life, but it was society that forced them to do it. I can't place the blame on anyone now or it would bother me forever. So I just blame it on society. Rachel is the one who started me thinking like this. At first, I disagreed with her philosophy, but now I think it's the healthiest way of looking at things. She really helped me a lot. That's because she knew how smart I was, how different. Every kid you have locked up here now is probably smarter than any of the other kids where they originally came from. That's why they got into trouble, because they were bored, and boredom is a killer disease. There was a girl from Winnetka, Illinois named Laurie Wasserman who went on a rampage and shot a bunch of children in their schoolhouse. Then she blew her own brains out because she was so bored with her miserable life. You probably heard about it on the news. Her married name was Laurie Dann. I knew her when she was in special education as a kid. It always seemed like she didn't know what to do to keep herself occupied. I'm sure she wanted to commit suicide for years, but didn't have the strength to do it until she killed somebody and knew she would be in jail for the rest of her life. She might have even done it just to get on TV. Geraldo Rivera did a horrible documentary about murder in America where he interviewed Charles Manson and showed actual footage of murders being committed, like the McDonald's massacre. When that show was on, I said to my wife, 'I bet someone will go berserk within the next week just to get on TV. They'll even make movies about it.' I had no idea it would happen so close to home. Laurie Dann had the potential to be one of the country's greatest mass murderers. Since it happened in Winnetka, though, most of her intended victims survived because of the excellent medical care and police action. Now, the Winnetka police have made a training film on the subject which sells for about five hundred dollars."

Elaine interjected, "I did hear about that on the news, and I understand what you're talking about. I think the media is partially to blame for the recent epidemic of murder in America. There's way too much violence on the open airwaves where anyone can see it."

I said with tongue in cheek, "I wish just once I'd turn on the TV and there'd be an announcement which said: 'Warning! The following program contains scenes of explicit sex!' instead of violence. I think our society would be much healthier if sex was shown more openly in the media. They've been doing it in Europe for years. It would provide a much-needed contrast to all the bullet-riddled corpses. The only breasts they'll show on TV here are those that have been chopped up and maimed... it's really weird. The bodies are piling up on our streets. Pretty soon our cities will be like South Africa unless somebody does something about it. We need a leader who will start taking serious action to make changes. I can't believe that after the Iran-Contra controversy, the public went ahead and voted the same damned administration into office! These people are crooks involved in a lot of shady dealings that we know nothing about, yet it's always the innocent civilians who get slaughtered because of their policies."

I could tell that Elaine was surprised by how much I had to say to her. I was attempting to condense ten years of personal philosophy into just ten minutes. She lit up a cigarette and offered me one, lighting it for me as a polite gesture. Then she cleared away all of her papers and documents and kicked her feet up onto her desk to relax while we talked further.

She asked, "Do you ever see any of the patients who were here when you were a patient?"

"Todd Darrel visited me in Chicago a few years ago, just for the hell of it. He's trying to push his own music like I am. If we weren't both lead singers and so egotistical, maybe we could have been in a band together. Last I heard, he was in Canada to promote his first record. I also saw Tara Baldwin recently when I went to Dayton, Ohio. I was just passing through on my way to see my old man in Athens, so I gave her a call and she invited me out to her house for a few days where we took care of some unfinished business. I believe she was married about a month ago."

I knew I should be on my way soon so that Elaine could get back to work, and I had a friend waiting for me in a van outside. I stood up from my chair like I was getting ready to leave, extinguishing my cigarette in the ashtray on her desk.

"Well, I couldn't travel through Topeka without stopping by to say hello. Talking with you now after all this time also helps me to reconcile the past, too. I'm glad I was able to personally bring everybody some of my records. Just be sure you play them loud for maximum enjoyment, all right?"

Elaine gave me another hug. "Thanks a lot. It was really great seeing you. I'll make sure Rachel gets these records with your address and phone number. I'm pretty sure Dr. Petersen knows how to reach her. Too bad he wasn't here today or you could have seen him, too. He's semi-retired now, though, ever since he suffered a heart attack."

"He had a heart attack?"

"Yes, but he made a remarkable recovery and he seems fine now. John, before you go I have just one more important question I'd like to ask you. If you had any advice that you could give to the troubled young people who are here now, what would it be? Take a minute to think about it if you want."

I could answer that right away. "Stand up for whatever you believe in and do whatever you want to do! I know that advice could get people in a lot of trouble with authority, but you can never really feel good about yourself unless you are happy with what you are doing in life. As long as you don't hurt anyone else, then the world is yours. Try to make it a better place, and maybe leave it a little cleaner than you found it. Set goals for yourself and achieve them, even if you don't have help from other people. The secret to life, I guess, is just to *live*. Don't sit around feeling sorry for yourself. Get out there and do something! Explore new horizons! After all, he who is not busy being born is busy dying!"

featherproof BOOKS

*Publishing strange and beautiful fiction and nonfiction
and post-, trans-, and inter-genre tragicomedy.*

Available at bookstores everywhere, and direct from Chicago, Illinois at
www.featherproof.com

Keep Up With The BESTSELLERS!

*fp*20 THE INBORN ABSOLUTE *by Robert Ryan* $60

This book collects the artist's past five years of Eastern deity paintings, mandala studies, and even an unfettered glimpse into his sketchbook. It also includes interviews with iconic performer and artist Genesis P. Orridge and legendary tattoo artist Freddy Corbin, which serve to contextualize Ryan's work and his progression as an artist.

*fp*18 THE TENNESSEE HIGHWAY DEATH CHANT *by Keegan Jennings Goodman* $13.95

Two teenagers are stranded in purgatory: Jenny wakes each morning, the same morning, and chronicles the events of her final day, her mind reaching back into the recesses of time, collecting a mythical past that bleeds into the details of her violent end. John drinks beer, philosophizes about the nature of reality and consciousness, and hurtles his Firebird Trans Am into the darkness beyond the headlights.

JNR170.3 ALL OVER AND OVER *by Tim Kinsella* $14.95

In 2003, living on constant tour through the dark days of the dawn of The War on Terror, Joan of Arc decided to regroup as a political hardcore band: Make Believe. For the next few years they maintained a grueling schedule. These are Kinsella's journals of their final, full U.S. tour—when he had to admit that the cost-benefit ratio of this lifestyle had toppled and he needed to stop.

*fp*16 ERRATIC FIRE, ERRATIC PASSION *by Jeff Parker & Pasha Malla* $14.95

The content of postgame interviews and sports chatter is often meaningless, if not insufferable. But some athletes transcend lame clichés and rote patter, using language in surprising, funny, and insightful ways. This book of "found" poems uses athletes' own words to celebrate those rare moments, with an introduction by award-winning sports writer Bethlehem Shoals.

*fp*15 SEE YOU IN THE MORNING *by Mairead Case* $13.95

Set one summer in a small Midwestern town, this book is about three 17-year-olds who take care of each other: Rosie, John, and the book's unnamed narrator, who works at a bookstore and sometimes focuses so hard on reading they see polka dots take over the room. This debut novel entangles the fraught intimacy, painful growth, and utter strangeness of youth in beautiful and lightning-bright prose.

fp14 THE FIRST COLLECTION OF CRITICISM BY A LIVING FEMALE ROCK CRITIC *by Jessica Hopper* $17.95

Jessica Hopper's music criticism has earned her a reputation as one of the firebrands of the form—a keen observer and fearless critic not just of music, but the culture around it, revealing new truths that often challenge us to consider what it is to be a fan. This book is a thoughtful document of the last 20 years of American music making and the shifting landscape of music consumption.

fp13 THE MINUS TIMES COLLECTED: TWENTY YEARS / THIRTY ISSUES (1992–2012) *edited by Hunter Kennedy* $16.95

Banged out on a 1922 Underwood typewriter, this 'zine began as an open letter to strangers and fellow misfits then grew into a breeding ground for the next generation of American fiction. Featuring Sam Lipsyte, Wells Tower, David Eggers, Dan Clowes, Barry Hannah, a yet-to-be-famous Stephen Colbert, and many more, with an introduction by Patrick DeWitt.

fp12 THE KARAOKE SINGER'S GUIDE TO SELF-DEFENSE *by Tim Kinsella* $14.95

Reunited for a funeral, a family finds dissonance in the fragments of their shared memories: a thoughtful dancer back at her bar, a bitter father working in a toothpaste factory, and a fist-fight addict struggling to keep his nose clean. Across town, a boy is locked up in a delusional man's home, and a teenage runaway looks for a new life in a strip club. Cruelty is a given. Karaoke is every Thursday.

fp11 THE UNIVERSE IN MINIATURE IN MINIATURE
by Patrick Somerville $14.95

In this genre-busting book of short stories we find a Chicago man who is bequeathed a supernatural helmet that allows him to experience the inner worlds of those around him; we peer into the mind of an art student grappling with ennui; we telescope out to the story of idiot extraterrestrials struggling to pilot a complicated spaceship; and we follow a retired mercenary as he tries to save his marriage and questions his life abroad.

fp10 DADDY'S by Lindsay Hunter $14.95

You ever fed yourself something bad? Like a candied rattlesnake, or a couple fingers of antifreeze? Nope? You seen what it done to other people? Like while they're flopping around on the floor, you're thinking about how they're fighting to live. Like while they're dying, they never looked so alive. That's what *Daddy's* is like.

fp09 THE AWFUL POSSIBILITIES by Christian TeBordo $14.95

A girl among kidney thieves masters the art of forgetting. A motivational speaker skins his best friend to impress his wife. A man outlines the rules and regulations for sadistic child-rearing. You've heard these people whispering in hallways, mumbling in diners, shouting in the apartment next door. In these stories, Christian TeBordo locates the awe in the awful possibilities we could never have imagined.

p08 SCORCH ATLAS *by Blake Butler* $14.95

A post-apocalyptic novel of 14 interlocking stories, set in ruined locales where birds speak gibberish, the sky rains gravel, and millions starve, disappear, or grow coats of mold. Rendered in beautiful language and in a variety of narrative forms, from a psychedelic fable to a skewed insurance claim questionnaire, Blake Butler's full-length fiction debut paints a gorgeously grotesque version of America.

fp07 AM/PM *by Amelia Gray* $12.95

If anything's going to save these characters from their troubled romances, their social improprieties, or their hands turning into claws, it's a John Mayer concert tee. This flash-fiction collection tours the lives of 23 characters across 120 stories full of lizard tails, Schrödinger boxes, and volcano love. It's an intermittent love story as seen through a darkly comic lens, mixing poetry and prose, humor and hubris.

fp05 BORING BORING BORING BORING BORING BORING BORING *by Zach Plague* $14.95

When the mysterious gray book that drives their twisted relationship goes missing, Ollister and Adelaide lose their post-modern marbles. He plots revenge against art patriarch The Platypus, while she obsesses over their anti-love affair. Meanwhile, the art school set experiments with bad drugs, bad sex, and bad ideas. This is a hybrid typo/graphic novel which skewers the art world, and those boring enough to fall into its traps.

*fp*04 THIS WILL GO DOWN ON YOUR PERMANENT RECORD *by Susannah Felts* $9.95

At the beginning of a lonely summer, 16-year-old Vaughn Vance meets Sophie Birch, and the two forge an instant and volatile alliance. When Vaughn takes up photography, she trains her lens on Sophie, and their bond dissolves as quickly as it came into focus. This YA novel illuminates the pitfalls of coming of age as an artist, the slippery nature of identity, and the clash of class in the New South.

*fp*03 HIDING OUT *by Jonathan Messinger* $13.95

This collection is filled with playful and empathic tales of misguided lonely hearts: A jilted lover dons robot armor to win back the heart of an ex-girlfriend; an angel loots the home of a single father; a teenager finds the key to everlasting life in a video game. Sparkling with humor and showcasing an array of styles, these characters dodge consequences while trying desperately to connect.

*fp*01 SONS OF THE RAPTURE *by Todd Dills* $12.95

Billy Jones and his dad have a score to settle. Up in Chicago, Billy drowns his past in booze. In South Carolina, his father saddles up for a drive to reclaim him. Caught in this perfect storm is a ragged assortment of savants: shape-shifting doctor, despairingly bisexual bombshell, tiara-crowned trumpeter, zombie senator.

THE ENCHANTERS VS. SPRAWLBURG SPRINGS
by Brian Costello $12.95

This novel is a satirical, riotous story of a band trapped in suburbia and bent on changing the world. A frenzied "scene" whips up around them as they gain popularity, and the band members begin thinking big. It's a hilarious, crazy send-up of self-destructive musicians, written in a prose filled with more music than anything on the radio today.